莱昂纳德·科恩 | 作品

LEONARD
COHEN

BOOK
OF
LONGING

中英对照 / 图文珍藏本

渴望之书

孔亚雷　北岛——译

上海译文出版社

献给欧文·莱顿
for Irving Layton

科恩的诗与歌
——代译序

孔亚雷

　　几张照片。透过一个圆环形的，具有六十年代风格，仿佛舷窗般的窗口（或者窥视孔），可以看见一个穿深色西装的男人。他既不年轻也不太老。他的西装很合身（就像一副优雅的盔甲）。他站在那儿——那儿看上去像个旅馆房间：打开的白色房门（球形门把手），拉了一半的落地窗帘（图案是繁复的花和枝蔓），从窗角涌入的光——朝右侧对着镜头，眼睛看着前方。不，你可以看出他其实什么都没看，他在沉思，一只手插在裤袋里，另一只手放在胸前，抚摩着自己的领带结。这是个回忆的姿势，回忆某个逝去的场景，并沉浸其中。他的脸上没有笑容。

　　另一张也是黑白的。但不像上一张那样泛黄（仿佛年代久远），场景也没有什么叙事感（他在回忆什么？）。它更像一张随意但独具风格的快照：一个穿深色条纹西装的男人，戴着墨镜，手里拿着一根吃了一半的香蕉（香蕉皮漂亮地奔拉下来）。背景是一间高大空旷类似LOFT的仓库。他面对镜头的角度几乎跟上一张一样，另一只手也插在口袋里（这次是上衣口袋），但这次他不像在思考或回忆，他只是在发呆，或者等待。（等待什么？某个女人？或者某个女人的命令？）跟上一张相比，他显得很放松，他看上去就像个心不在焉的黑手党。他的体形已经不再锋利，他的西装仍然很优雅，但已经不像盔甲而更像浴袍（西装里

1

面是白色的圆领衫）。无所谓，他似乎在说，没什么好想的，随他们去。他没有笑。

而这一张——第一眼看上去不像照片。哦——你很快就会发现——那是某种Photoshop的电脑效果。油画效果，那叫。两个人的脸部特写占据了整个画面，一个老头和年轻女人。整个背景都虚成了淡蓝色，那种暮色刚刚降临时的淡蓝，他们并排着，从那片蓝色中浮现出来：发梢，鬓角，皱纹。V字领、白衬衫、条纹领带。就像一帧剪影。照例，他（以及她）侧对着我们（这次是朝左），视线微微向下。那个女人在微笑。那个老头呢？很难说。他似乎在以极小的幅度微笑（嘴角涌起长长的皱纹），但同时又眉头微锁（似乎在追随某种节奏）。是的，他们给人一种正在跳舞的感觉，无论是身体还是心。你仿佛能听到柔缓的鼓点响起，音乐像淡蓝的暮色那样弥漫，然后，他开始唱。

他开始唱——我不知不觉按下了书架音响的PLAY键。那三张照片就摆在旁边的书桌上。当然，它们不是真正的照片，它们是三张CD封面。我最爱的三张莱昂纳德·科恩的唱片：《精选集》（*THE BEST OF LEONARD COHEN*），《我是你的男人》（*I'M YOUR MAN*），《十首新歌》（*TEN NEW SONGS*）。这三张唱片几乎概括了他的大半生。三十三岁之前，他依次是早年丧父的富家公子（他九岁时父亲去世），加拿大才华横溢的青年诗人（他二十二岁出版了第一部诗集，《让我们跟神话比比》），隐居希腊海岛的前卫小说家（两本意识流风格的小说，《至爱游戏》和《美丽失败者》）。而在三十三岁之后，他依次成为纽约的民谣歌手（住在波普圣地切尔西旅馆，抱着吉他自编自弹自唱），迷倒众生的情歌王子（据说他的唱片法国女人人手一张），南加利福尼亚秃山上的禅宗和尚（主要任务是每天给老师做饭），以及——不可避免地——一个老头。

事实上，他似乎从未年轻过。漫长而优雅的苍老绵延了他的整个艺术生命。（这也许正是为什么他越来越迷人，越来越受欢迎的原因，如果作品——音乐，文学，表演，等等——的光芒来源于年轻，那光芒就会日渐黯淡，因为你会越来越不年轻；而如果相反，作品的光芒来源于苍老，它就会日益明亮，因为你会越来越老。）以上面的三张唱片为界，他的苍老可以分为三个阶段：首先是回忆。正如《精选集》封面上那个手抚领带的姿态所暗示的，科恩早期的歌曲充满了回忆，回忆过去（希腊，旧爱，甚至旧情敌），偶尔提及现在（酒，寂寞，纽约的冷），但从不提未来（似乎未来毫无意义，或者根本不存在）。那是一种带着苍老感的回忆，平静，忧伤，经过克制的一丝绝望。比如《苏珊娜》《别了，玛丽安娜》，以及那首著名的《著名的蓝雨衣》。听这些歌，你仿佛能看见一片雪地，看见素描般的黑色树枝，看见小小音符般的"电线上的鸟"——那也是他的一首歌名。

然后是无所谓。既然——反正——越来越老。无所谓得，也无所谓失；无所谓将来，也无所谓过去。他已经懒得去回忆。他当然也懒得去反抗，懒得去愤怒，懒得去争抢。他甚至懒得去绝望。他已经看穿了这个世界，这个无聊虚伪充满暴力争名夺利的世界。他就像个退休的黑手党（那张戴墨镜吃香蕉的唱片封面就是最好的写照），已经厌倦了打打杀杀的生涯，决定投靠另一个老大：他所爱的女人。因为一切都没有意义。一切都不值一提。除了一件事——爱情。那就是莱昂纳德·科恩式的情歌。苍老而柔美，毫不激烈，毫无保留，把所有的情感与尊严都倾于自己深爱的女人，正如他流传最广的那首歌的歌名：《我是你的男人》（它以小小的、谦虚的黑体印在唱片封面那张黑手党快照的上方）。如果你想要个爱人，他在歌中唱道（用一种近乎喃喃自语的低沉声调），我会对你百依百顺/如果你想要不一样的爱/我会为你戴上面具/如果你想要个舞伴/请牵我的手/或者如果你发火想把我揍趴下/我就在这儿/我是你的男人。我是你的男人。他不停重复着这句话，像是一种咒语，一种哀求，或者，一种祈祷。

然后他继续唱，也继续老。直到有一天他突然感到厌倦——厌倦了唱，也厌倦了老。1994年，六十岁的他——已经是个真正意义上的老人——在南加州秃山上的禅修中心，开始了长达五年的隐居修行。不久，他正式成为禅宗和尚，法号"自闲"。（具有讽刺意味的是，作为对以往人生的一种告别，"自闲"意为"沉默的一个"。）正是禅宗，以其特有的**为所欲为**，赋予了科恩式苍老新的活力。一种生气勃勃的苍老，一种因为放下自我而变得无所不能的苍老。他开始微笑，开始跳舞，一切都变得自然而然，就像风，就像溪流，就像一棵树或一朵云。五年之后，当他带着皮箱里的近千首诗歌，从山林回到城市，一如孔子所说，年近七十的老科恩已经"七十而从心所欲，不逾矩"。于是2001年，我们有了《十首新歌》。封面上出现了久违的色彩（一片如同暮色般的蓝色，一抹令人想起晚霞的昏黄），久违的笑意，以及久违的女人（他的伴唱，莎朗·罗宾森）。他开始继续唱——或者不如说在低声吟诵——"我们依然做爱，在我的秘密人生"，"我老了，但我依然陷入，一千个吻那么深"。他的声音变得更苍老，更深情，仿佛已经没有火焰的温暖炉火。（苍老使他的深情更加无所畏惧，无所顾忌，同时也无所匹敌，因为苍老对于矫情——深情最容易染上的毛病——有天生的免疫力。）他变得更自由，更轻盈，现在他可以自如地面对一切，通过释放一切——不管那是衰老，死亡，还是情欲。所以2006，七十二岁的莱昂纳德·科恩，坦白地——同时不无狡猾和骄傲地——把自己的新诗集（它们大多来自从秃山带下的那个皮箱）命名为《渴望之书》。

这本书现在就摆在我面前。一年多以来，它每天都陪在我身边。必须承认，如果不是因为他的歌，我们也许不会去读他的诗。这很难说是好是坏。一方面，正是那些美妙的歌把我们领向了这些同样美妙的诗。（另一位诗人，挪威老头奥夫拉·H.豪格，就没这么幸运，虽然他的诗跟科恩的一样迷人，我向你强烈推荐他的诗集中译本《我站着，我受得了》。）而另一方面，他作为歌手的光芒如此耀眼，以至于他的诗和小

4

说很容易被忽略（就像我们忽略贝克特的诗和罗伯－格里耶的电影）。
不过，不管怎样，我们的老科恩似乎都无所谓——出于谦逊，出于禅宗
式的无我，出于深深的、无名的寂寞，正如他那首名为《头衔》的诗所
写的：

我有诗人的头衔

或许有一阵子

我是个诗人

我也被仁慈地授予

歌手的头衔

尽管

我几乎连音都唱不准

有好多年

我被大家当成和尚

我剃了光头，穿上僧袍

每天起得很早

我讨厌每个人

却装得很宽容

结果谁也没发现

我那大众情人的名声

是个笑话

它让我只能苦笑着

度过一万个

孤单的夜晚

从葡萄牙公园旁边

三楼的一扇窗户

我看着雪

下了一整天

一如往常

这儿一个人也没有

从来都没有

幸好

冬天的白噪音

消除了

内心的对话

也消除了

"我既不是思想，

智慧，

也不是内在的沉默之音……"

那么，敬爱的读者

你以什么名义

以谁的名义

来跟我一起

在这奢侈

每况愈下

无所事事的隐居王国中

 闲逛？

　　闲逛。难道这不是对读诗这一行为——多么无用的行为——绝妙而形象的比喻？而我又是以什么名义，在科恩先生那冷幽默，无政府，充满禅意的隐居王国中，毫无节制地闲逛呢？回答是：以一个译者的名义，或者，更抽象一点，以爱的名义。

　　2009年秋天的那个下午，接到邀请我翻译科恩诗集的电话时，我几乎毫不犹豫就答应下来。回想起来，我至今还感到后怕（但不后悔）。

我竟然无视两个最明显的障碍：首先，诗是**不可能翻译的**（诗就是在翻译中丢失的东西——美国大诗人罗伯特·弗罗斯特说）；其次，我不是诗人（只有诗人才有资格翻译诗——我忘了是谁说的）。一向理智（或者你也可以说怯懦）的我，为什么会做出这样鲁莽的决定呢？唯一的解释就是爱。对科恩歌曲的爱。对科恩苍老的爱。说不清到底为什么的爱（我将在后面试着说清楚一点）。因此，当我译到下面这首小诗，我不禁发出会心的微笑（苦笑）。

老人和蔼。

年轻人愤怒。

爱也许盲目。

但欲望却不。

——《老人的悲哀》

因此也许可以说，这本译作的诞生源自爱，而不是欲望。这也是我个人对婚姻和工作（写小说和翻译）的态度。一切都应当**发源于爱**，而非欲望，不是吗？但经验也告诉我们，就过程和成绩而言，最好的效果往往产生于爱与欲望的结合。**爱也许盲目，但欲望却不。**对于婚姻，那会产生一个可爱的孩子；对于写作，那会产生一部美妙的作品。而具体到这本书，这本因为一种盲目的爱而开始的书，我有一个非常明确的欲望：尽可能把它译好。

我花了近一年半时间翻译这部《渴望之书》。其间写了几篇短篇小说（它们后来被收进名为《火山旅馆》的一部小说集里），也在为新长篇做准备（读书，做笔记，锻炼身体）。除周末外，大部分时间我都一个人待在莫干山上的一座石头房子里。清晨——我一般六点起床——在厨房煮咖啡的时候，从窗口可以看见院子里的月季和远处的群山。自然，这种生活经常让我想起科恩在诗中常提到的秃山。自然，我也能深切体会到他那散发着黑色幽默的孤单。

> 我剃光了头
>
> 我穿上僧袍
>
> 我睡在一间小木屋的角落
>
> 在六千五百英尺的山上
>
> 这儿很凄凉
>
> 我唯一不需要的
>
> 就是梳子
>
> ——《害相思病的和尚》

但孤独是必需的，无论是对一个和尚，还是一个作家。无论是对修行，还是对写作。对于写作，孤独就像纸笔（或者电脑）、才华和耐心一样必不可少。你只能一个人写（或者翻译）。所以，制造出这本译作的，除了盲目的爱，明确的欲望，还应该加上无边的孤单。此外，值得一提的是，虽然众所周知，翻译诗歌极为困难和不讨巧，但就这本书而言，它有一个特别的优势：它是中英对照版。（一个朋友——也是位诗人——在听到这个消息后宣称，世界上所有的翻译诗集都应该是双语对照版。）因为当然，我的译文不可能比原文更好，而且我也可以自豪地——虽然出版中英对照跟我并没有关系——对我同样热爱和尊重的罗伯特·弗罗斯特先生说，您瞧，诗没有丢，它还在那儿。

又一张照片。它是我在一个叫"莱昂纳德·科恩档案"的网站上发现的。这个网站的网址，www.leonardcohenfiles.com，被列在《渴望之书》最后一页致谢名单的第一段。《渴望之书》中的许多诗和画作，最早都发表在这个芬兰网站。点开蓝色主页左侧栏目列表中的Articles and Interviews（报道与访谈），你立刻就会看见这张照片——《香巴拉太阳》杂志1998年9月号的封面照。拍的是两个和尚（两个老和尚）。

在禅室中（书法，白墙，杯钵）。一坐一立。坐着的这位，嘴角下拉，表情严厉（但似乎是装的，就像大人在跟小孩开玩笑），他把脸别向左侧，眼睛故意不看镜头（似乎在说"我才懒得看你"）。他就是科恩在书中常常写到——也画到（也是这副表情）——的"老师"：杏山禅师。站在他身后的当然就是科恩。不，应该叫自闲。这是一个新科恩，一个新老头，跟以往的形象完全不同：他留着几乎是光头的短发（颜色花白）；他的站姿恭敬而谦卑；他的眼睛直视镜头；更重要的是，他的脸上流露出一种孩子般顽皮而可爱的笑容，而且似乎在忍着不让自己笑得太明显，似乎他刚刚犯了什么错（干了什么恶作剧），似乎他本该低下眼睛，现在却忍不住要偷偷看上一眼。还有衣服。他和老师都身着古老雅致的僧袍。至于僧袍的具体样式，科恩在一首诗中为我们做了很好的描述：

闹钟凌晨2：30把我叫醒：

我穿上僧袍

和服和褶裙

式样仿自12世纪

弓术家的装束：

再外面是海青

一件厚重的外衣

袖子奇大无比：

再外面是挂络

一种碎布拼成的围兜

上面系着一块象牙色圆环：

最后是四英尺长

蛇一般蜿蜒的腰带

打成一个巨大漂亮的结

像块绞成辫形的哈拉面包*

绑在挂络后面：

总共这些

大概20磅重的衣服

我在凌晨2：30

辉煌的勃起中

快速穿上

——《秃山的清晨》

    我们很难想象，以前的科恩会在他的诗或歌中如此直接地提到"勃起"这个词。早在1984年，科恩出版过另一本带有强烈宗教感的诗集，其中的诗篇在很大程度上受到《圣经》和犹太教律法书的影响，因而被称为"当代赞美诗"（科恩本人则认为它们是一种"祈祷"）。与《渴望之书》形成鲜明对比的是，那部诗集的标题叫《仁慈之书》。所以，如果说西方宗教是在教我们如何仁慈地去面对这个世界，那么禅宗就在教我们如何坦诚地去面对这个世界，并且在禅宗看来，那实际上也就是如何坦诚地面对自己（因为世界和"我"已经融为一体），面对自己的存在、自己的消失和自己的渴望。这种坦诚，说到底，是一种终极的超脱，它也体现在禅宗对于自身的态度上，禅宗甚至根本不把自己当成一种宗教——虽然当了禅宗和尚，但作为一名犹太人，科恩仍旧是个虔诚的犹太教徒。当《纽约时报》的记者问他如何在这两者间保持一致时，他回答说："好多年前艾伦·金斯伯格也问过我同样的问题……首先，在我练习的禅宗传统里，没有虔诚的崇拜，也没有一个确定的神灵。所以理论上这对任何犹太信仰都不构成威胁。"的确，在《渴望之书》里，我们看不到虔诚的崇拜（他和老师一起喝酒——结果被灌醉；他给<u>老师放重要的黄色录像——结果老师看睡着了</u>，并在醒来后说"研究人

*哈拉面包（challah），犹太教在安息日或其他假日食用的一种辫形或麻花形面包。

类的爱很有意思，但也不是那么有意思"），也看不到确定的神灵（信上帝/真的很好玩/什么时候你一定要试试/现在就试/看看上帝/是不是/想让你/信他），我们只看到生命的坦然。那是一种禅宗所特有的，近乎天真的（但绝不幼稚），孩子般的坦然。如果我们要用一种表情来形容这些诗和画，那么毫无疑问，那就是科恩与杏山禅师合影上所露出的老顽童式的笑容。它们带着恶作剧的幽默，清澈的智慧，以及由于摆脱了时间和焦虑控制的自在与喜悦。就像下面这几首奇妙的、俳句般的小诗：

每次我告诉他
接下来我想干什么，
莱顿就严肃地问：
莱昂纳德，你确定
你做的是错的吗？
——《莱顿的问题》

亲爱的，现在我有个黄油杯
形状做得像奶牛
——《黄油杯》

月亮在外面。
刚才我去小便的时候
看见了这个伟大而简洁的东西。
我应该看得再久一点。
我是个可怜的月亮爱好者。
我突然就看见了它
对我和月亮

都是这样。

　　　　——《月亮》

我做爱时作弊

她觉得很棒

她给我看

你只会给作弊者

看的东西

　　　　——《作弊》

　　在《作弊》这首诗下方，有一张小小的、妖冶的黑白裸女画。而在《月亮》下方，有两张稍大一点的画，一张是禅味十足的竹枝和月亮，一张是一朵梅花和科恩头像。在点缀书间的近百幅手绘小画中，占据前三位的主题依次为：自画像（大多很丑），裸女（丰乳肥臀），老师（样子很拽）。只要稍加观察，你就会发现——相对应地，那也是这部诗集最重要的三个主题：自我（丑陋的），欲望（旺盛的），禅宗（严厉的）。这三个主题是相互关联的。所有宗教都为了同一个目的而存在：解决做人的痛苦。禅宗也不例外（在广义上它仍然是一种宗教）。而人的痛苦主要来自两方面：精神和物质，或者具体一点，自我和欲望。但与所有其他宗教不同的是，禅宗提出的解决方法独具一格，甚至可以说绝无仅有：它主张面对，而不是逃避；它主张陶醉，而不是忍耐；它主张当机立断，而不是沉思冥想；它主张融入当下，而不是寄望来世；它主张依靠自己，而不是祈求神灵。更奇特的是，它战胜对手的手段不是打倒对手，而是拥抱对手。那种拥抱放肆而放松，有力而无心，瞬间而永恒，于是一切都融为一个不可分割的整体，于是也就无所谓——不存在——什么对手，什么成败，什么生死。于是自我变成无我。欲望变成希望。悖论成为真理。在禅宗声东击西的指引下（当然它会否认有过任何指引），我们进入了一个新世界，一个真正的**勇敢新世界**（跟赫胥黎笔下的完全不同）。

《渴望之书》，就是老科恩在那个新世界的笔记。

所以我们的老科恩开始勇敢地——放松而放肆地——拥抱他的自我和欲望。在那些线条狂野的自画像旁边，有这样一些手写的句子：生气勃勃/但已经死了；脸可以被画得看上去一点都不蠢/但却不平衡得吓人；发火，晚上11点；感觉不错；我们不会整场演出都待在那儿；我一直没找到那个女孩/我一直没发财/跟我学。而我觉得最有趣（也最有代表性）的是下面两条：担心，当然/失败，当然/老了，当然/感恩，当然/自从/背景/消失以后；以及还在看女孩/但根本/没有女孩/一个都没有/只有（这会害死你）/内心的平静/与和谐。

所以在一个《心乱之晨》，面对自己的欲望，他表现出几乎令人伤感的直白：

> 啊。那。
> 那就是我这个早晨
> 如此心乱的原因：
> 我的欲望回来了，
> 我再一次想要你。
> 我做得很好，
> 我超然面对一切。
> 男孩和女孩们都很美丽
> 而我是个老人，爱着每个人。
> 但现在我再一次想要你，
> 想要你全部的注意，
> 想要你的内裤迅速滑落
> 还挂在一只脚上，

而我脑海一片空白
只想着要到
那唯一的里面
那里
没有里，
　　　也没有外。

所以他开始抖落那些现成的框架和概念——就像在阳光下抖落僧袍上的灰尘——用更动物性，更直观，更接近孩童的方法去解决问题：

我从未真正听懂
他说的话
但时不时地
我发现自己
在跟狗一起叫
　跟鸢尾花一起弯腰
或用其他的小方式
排忧解难
　　　——《老师》

所以悖论成为真理（唯一的）：成功就是失败，失败也就是成功。学禅就是不学禅，学成就是学不成。在一首《禅的崩溃》中，他以一段充满欲望的场景开始：

我可以把脸
塞进那个地方
跟我的呼吸搏斗

当她垂下热切的手指

　　打开自己，

好让我用整个嘴

解除她的饥渴，

　　她最隐秘的饥渴——

我何必还要开悟？

　　我何必还要开悟？科恩在诗中不断地反问（就像反复出现的主音旋律），直到诗的最后两行：我何必在开悟的祭坛上瑟瑟发抖？／我何必要永远保持笑容？当他最终在五年后《离开秃山》，他干脆坦然承认：我最终明白了／我不是修行的料。（或许这正是修行成功——至少在某种意义上——的标志？）而当他回到万丈红尘，《向R.S.B.汇报》（R.S.B是Ramesh S.Balsekar的缩写，印度圣人萨伽达塔·马哈拉吉的门徒，著名的不二论哲学大师），则用一种充满自嘲的"无我"总结了他的禅修成果：

平静没有进入我的生活。

我的生活逃走了

　　而平静还在那儿。

我常常碰见我的生活，

当它想歇口气，

付账单，

或忍受那些新闻，

当它一如既往

被某人

　　美的缆绳绊倒——

我小小的生活：

如此忠诚
如此执着于它那模糊的目标——
而且，我急忙汇报说，
没有我也干得很好。

　　没错，这是个新的世界，有新的光线，但它并没有失去旧世界的美好。它只是让原有的美好显得更加轮廓鲜明，更加毫无矫饰。因为无论从什么角度看，禅宗都更像一种自然而然的过渡和延续，而非某种人为的侵入或纠正。它就像晨光，暮色，花开，月亮，是在几乎无法被意识到的时间之流里不知不觉地发生。因此，当我们这些被科恩歌声吸引而来的人，当我们在这座禅园般的隐居王国里闲逛（无论是以译者的名义还是粉丝的名义），我们不会感到有任何陌生或不适。他还是我们亲爱的老科恩。不管身着西装还是僧袍，他那迷人的招牌式苍老都依然如故——不，也许更自然，更简洁，更深邃。他依然回忆：

我坐在这张桌旁
大约四十年前
那些歌
正是从这里开始——
忙碌得像只
寂寞的蜜蜂
　　　　——《餐桌》

他依然无所谓：

时光感觉多么甜蜜
当一切都太晚

当你不必再跟随

她摇曳的臀部

一路进入

你饥渴的想像

——《甜蜜时光》

他依然失落：

我和树叶一起走路

我和铬一起发亮

我几乎还活着

我几乎很舒服

没人可追随

没东西可教

除了一点：目标

不可能达到

——《目标》

他依然渴望：

今天早晨上帝打开我的眼睛

松开睡眠的绷带

让我看见

那个女侍者的小耳环

和她的小乳房

——《打开我的眼睛》

当然，他也依然情深款款。在这里，科恩写下了也许是世界上最简洁，最深情，也最动人的情诗，它仿佛是那首《我是你的男人》的遥远回声，正如诗的标题——《最甜蜜的短歌》——所暗示的，它只有短短两行：

你走你的路
我也走你的路

*

我第一次听科恩的歌是在2003年1月。我记得这么清楚是因为几乎就在同时，我辞去了报社的工作（当时我是书评版编辑），决定全力以赴——在三十岁来临之前——写出自己的第一部小说。那年我二十八岁。我在一个朋友，一个先锋音乐家的旧公寓里（里面的唱片堆积如山）听到了那张《十首新歌》。（也许是某种巧合，也是在这个朋友家里，在他的唱片堆里，我找到了我第一部小说的名字：不失者——它是日本实验音乐家灰野敬二的一个乐队组合。）我立刻迷上了科恩。就像对我迷上的其他那些作家（比如让·艾什诺兹）、歌手（比如比莉·哈乐黛）和导演（比如大卫·林奇）一样，我开始四处搜寻科恩的作品。不久——大概半年后——我就拥有了他的大部分CD，包括我在文章开头提到的那三张（大多是在杭州翠苑夜市卖原版唱片的地摊上淘到的，可惜这个夜市现在已经消失）。

虽然我做出辞职写作的决定跟听到科恩的歌并没有直接关系，但现在回想起来，科恩的歌，科恩的歌声，显然使我更加坚定了自己的决心——或许是在下意识里。那也解释了，为什么我在辞职后写的第一篇文章不是小说，而是一篇小小的，关于莱昂纳德·科恩的乐评。那篇乐评的标题是：《我老了》。

我老了。也许那就是我决定辞职的原因。也许那就是我——天真而偏执地——想在三十岁之前写一部小说的原因。我不想再浪费生命。我开始意识到我只有一次生命，而且它不可能重来。我必须抓住这唯一的机会，去做我想做的事（对我来说那就是写小说）。所以在我听来，科恩那苍老醇厚的歌声，仿佛是一种温暖的安慰和鼓舞。你只能活一次，他仿佛在说，所以要用全部力量，去爱你所爱的人，去做你想做的事。

我开始经常听他的歌，特别是在写《不失者》那段时间。我总在傍晚听，在吃完晚饭，结束一天的工作之后。坐在沙发上，一边喝廉价葡萄酒一边大脑一片空白地听。与其说是听音乐不如说在发呆。回过神来，房间里往往已经一片黑暗，而歌声听上去就像是黑暗本身在唱。有种安宁而充实的幸福感。就像被包裹在一个茧里面。你被茧里的黑暗（以及黑暗中的歌声）保护着。你知道自己在做正确的事——做你想做的事，而且会把它做好。

所以也许这很自然——甚至可以说必然——在《不失者》的一个场景里出现了科恩的歌（就像电影原声那样，这是小说原声）。不过，我并不是刻意要那样做。只是在写到那个部分时，我突然觉得那样的场景**应该**配上科恩的音乐。那是个面对死亡的场景，或者说，临死之前的场景（虽然跟世界上大部分小说的主人公一样，最后他并没有死）。为了更好地说明这个场景（为了更好地说明*我对科恩盲目的爱*），请允许我用一句话概括一下《不失者》的故事：一个普通的都市白领，有一天忽然发现自己是名**不失者**——出于某种特殊的商业利益，他的人生（记忆，工作，生活）完全受控于某个庞大的神秘组织，于是为了找回失去的记忆，为了追寻真正的自我（就像侦探小说里的追查真凶），他踏上了一场诡异的逃亡之旅（就像公路电影那样奇遇不断）。这个场景发生在故事的一半。主人公（以及一个女孩）本想逃入深山，但由于进山的道路被泥石流堵住，所以他们决定——也只能——在羁留的海边小镇上静静地等死。一对年轻男女，肩并肩坐在防波堤上，面对深夜月光下的大海，一首接一首地听着科恩，像等待天亮一样等待着死亡的光临。

就是那样的场景。

虽然写的时候并没有多想，但现在看回去（就在我写这篇文章的现在，此刻），我似乎突然发现了一个秘密。一个关于科恩的秘密。一个关于我对科恩"盲目的爱"的谜底。为什么我会那样本能地，自然而然地为那个场景配上科恩的音乐呢？那个场景有什么特别之处呢？答案——或者说秘密——就是死。也许在我们的内心深处，在我们的潜意识里，科恩的歌——或者可以扩大一点，科恩的诗与歌——让我们想到死。感觉到死。它们是面对死亡的诗与歌。它们并不抵抗，也不逃避，只是平静地，甚至温柔地凝望。凝望着无所不在，仿佛暗夜般的死亡。但那黑暗并不可怕。或者说，并没有我们想象的那么可怕。科恩的歌好像在告诉我们，黑暗也可以是一种保护，一层温暖的茧。死也一样。死也可以是一种保护，一种温暖的限制。我们常常都忘了自己会死，不是吗？所以我们才会成为不失者。所以我们才会糟蹋自己好不容易才轮到的人生。所以才有政治和战争，欺骗和罪恶。是死在保护我们。提醒我们。教导我们。教我们珍惜，教我们勇敢，教我们去爱，去劳动，去创造艺术。去怎样真正活着。

对，我想这就是我如此热爱科恩的原因，这就是为什么六年后的一个下午，我会毫不犹豫地答应翻译这本《渴望之书》。

致　谢

感谢我的编辑冯涛和路佳瑄，没有他们，就没有您手上的这本书。

感谢北岛，没有他的慷慨参与，这本书会失色不少。*

感谢莫干山THE LODGE咖啡馆的Emily（爱美丽），没有她耐心而温柔的帮助，这本书中会出现更多可笑而可怕的错误。

感谢上海的Arthur Jones（罗飞），理由同上。

再次感谢Arthur Jones（罗飞），感谢他在笔记本上为我写下Bob Dylan（鲍勃·迪伦）的那句话：The only thing I knew how to do was to keep on keeping on.（我惟一知道怎么做的事，就是坚持我的坚持。）

感谢我的家人叶全新，孔祥彪，叶芽，楼莺和孔象象，没有他们就没有一切（对我来说）。

2011年3月，莫干山

渴望之书

我进不了深山
那系统不灵
我依赖药片
还得感谢上天

我沿那路程
从混乱到艺术
欲望为马
抑郁为车

我像天鹅航行
我像石头下沉
而时光远去
不理我的笑柄

我的纸太白
我的墨太淡

白昼不肯写下
夜用铅笔涂鸦

我的动物嚎叫
我的天使不安
却不许我
有丝毫悔怨

而有人将会
强我所难
我的心属于他
处之淡然

她将踏上小路
知我所言
我的意志切成两半
在自由之间

转瞬片刻
我们生命会相撞
那无尽的停摆
那敞开的门

而她将为你
这样的人诞生
敢为人先
继续向前

我知道她正到来
我知道她将顾盼
就是那渴望
就是这书

(北岛　译)

1

I can't make the hills
The system is shot
I'm living on pills
For which I thank G-d

I followed the course
From chaos to art
Desire the horse
Depression the cart

I sailed like a swan
I sank like a rock
But time is long gone
Past my laughing stock

My page was too white
My ink was too thin
The day wouldn't write
What the night pencilled in

My animal howls
My angel's upset
But I'm not allowed
A trace of regret

For someone will use
What I couldn't be
My heart will be hers
Impersonally

She'll step on the path
She'll see what I mean
My will cut in half
And freedom between

For less than a second
Our lives will collide
The endless suspended
The door open wide

Then she will be born
To someone like you
What no one has done
She'll continue to do

I know she is coming
I know she will look
And that is the longing
And this is the book

穿僧袍的生活

过了一会儿
你分不出
是在思念
一个女人
还是需要
一根香烟
然后
这是夜晚
还是白天
接着突然
你知道了
时间
你穿衣
　回家
　点烟
　结婚

MY LIFE IN ROBES

After a while
You can't tell
If it's missing
A woman
Or needing
A cigarette
And later on
If it's night
Or day
Then suddenly
You know
The time
You get dressed
You go home
You light up
You get married

主人之声*

听完莫扎特
（我经常听）
我总要
扛着一架钢琴
在秃山
爬上爬下
我不是说
电子琴
我是说一架真正大小
水泥做的
三角钢琴
既然我快要死了
我就一步
也不后悔

HIS MASTER'S VOICE

After listening to Mozart
(which I often did)
I would always
Carry a piano
Up and down
Mt. Baldy
And I don't mean
A keyboard
I mean a full-sized
Grand piano
Made of cement
Now that I am dying
I don't regret
A single step

---

*英国古董手摇唱机品牌，标识即是只著名的小狗。

老师89

老师*很累，
　　他躺在床上
他和活着的一起活着
　　和死去的一起死去
但现在他想再喝一杯
　　（惊奇永远不断？）
他向战争开战
　　他也向和平开战
他坐在宝殿中
　　露出伟大的真面目
他向无开战
　　无中有深意
他的胃口很不错
　　那些李子挺有用
没人去天堂
　　也没人留在地狱

　　　　——秃山，1996

ROSHI AT 89

Roshi's very tired,
　　he's lying on his bed
He's been living with the living
　　and dying with the dead
But now he wants another drink
　　(will wonders never cease?)
He's making war on war
　　and he's making war on peace
He's sitting in the throne-room
　　on his great Original Face
and he's making war on Nothing
　　that has Something in its place
His stomach's very happy
　　The prunes are working well
There's no one going to Heaven
　　and there's no one left in Hell

　　　　　　　– *Mt. Baldy, 1996*

* 老师，即佐佐木承周，又称杏山禅师，秃山禅修中心的创办人。

我的一封信

我跟一位有名的拉比通信
但师父瞥见了我写的一封信
他制止了我。
"亲爱的拉比,"我最后一次给他写道,
"我没有资格或者悟性
谈论这些事情。
我只是在卖弄。
请原谅我。
你的犹太兄弟,
自闲·埃利泽*。"

ONE OF MY LETTERS

I corresponded with a famous rabbi
but my teacher caught sight of one of my letters
and silenced me.
"Dear Rabbi," I wrote him for the last time,
"I do not have the authority or understanding
to speak of these matters.
I was just showing off.
Please forgive me.
Your Jewish brother,
Jikan Eliezer."

---

*科恩1996年在秃山禅修中心正式成为禅宗和尚,法号"自闲"。

你也会唱

你也会唱
要是你发现自己
在一个像这样的地方
你不会担心
自己有没有
雷·查尔斯或伊迪丝·琵雅芙*
那么棒
你会唱
你会唱
不是为你自己
而是为造出一个自己
从烂在星形肠子里的
旧食物
从你自己呼吸中
无爱的怦然心动
你会成为一名歌手
快得来不及
去怨恨对手的魅力
你会唱，亲爱的
你也会唱

You'd Sing Too

You'd sing too
if you found yourself
in a place like this
You wouldn't worry about
whether you were as good
as Ray Charles or Edith Piaf
You'd sing
You'd sing
not for yourself
but to make a self
out of the old food
rotting in the astral bowel
and the loveless thud
of your own breathing
You'd become a singer
faster than it takes
to hate a rival's charm
and you'd sing, darling
you'd sing too

---

* 雷·查尔斯 (Ray Charles)，美国著名黑人歌手，被称为"灵魂歌王"；伊迪丝·琵雅芙 (Edith Piaf)，法国传奇女歌手，被称为"法国云雀"。

S.O.S. 1995

在你的愤怒上多花点时间，
懒鬼。
别浪费它去闹事。
别让它跟意念纠缠。
魔鬼不许我说，
只准我暗示
你是个奴隶，
你在他们的奴役下受罪
你的苦难是他们蓄意的策略，
你的不幸
是他们的养分。
那边是暴行，
这边是内心的麻痹——
想要更好的待遇？
你被严格约束。
你被饲养以用来痛苦。
魔鬼拴住了我的舌头。
我跟你说，
"我潦草人生的朋友"
你已被那些人征服
他们懂得如何暗中去征服
幕帘飘动得多么美丽，

蕾丝幕帘背后
某个甜蜜古老的阴谋：
魔鬼在引诱我
不再向你发出警报。
所以我得说快点：
你的生命中不管是谁，
那些伤害你的，
那些帮助你的，
那些你认识的
和那些你不认识的——
让他们解脱
帮他们解脱
认清那解脱。
您正在收听的是"反抗电台"。

S.O.S. 1995

Take a long time with your anger,
sleepyhead.
Don't waste it in riots.
Don't tangle it with ideas.
The Devil won't let me speak,
will only let me hint
that you are a slave,
your misery a deliberate policy
of those in whose thrall you suffer,
and who are sustained
by your misfortune.
The atrocities over there,
the interior paralysis over here –
Pleased with the better deal?
You are clamped down.
You are being bred for pain.
The Devil ties my tongue.
I'm speaking to you,
'friend of my scribbled life.'
You have been conquered by those
who know how to conquer invisibly.
The curtains move so beautifully,
lace curtains of some
sweet old intrigue:
the Devil tempting me
to turn away from alarming you.
So I must say it quickly:
Whoever is in your life,
those who harm you,
those who help you;
those whom you know
and those whom you do not know –
let them off the hook,
help them off the hook.
Recognize the hook.
You are listening to Radio Resistance.

当我喝酒

当我和老师
喝着
300美元的苏格兰威士忌
它解除了所有的渴
一首歌来到我的唇边
一个女人和我躺在一起
而每个欲望
都邀我蜷起赤裸的身体
进入它滴着口水的嘴里

不能喝了，我大叫，不能喝了
但老师又倒满了我的杯子
新的激情给了我
新的胃口
比如说
我掉进了一朵郁金香
（而且一直没有掉到底）
或在夜晚狂飙
跟某个有北斗七星
两倍大的人
汗津津地性交

当我和老师一起吃肉
四只脚的动物

不再嚎叫
两只脚的动物
不想飞走
筋疲力尽的鲑鱼
游回我手心
而老师的狼
咬着它断掉的锁链
跟每个人都成了朋友
这在小屋
引起了轰动

当我和老师一起大快朵颐
当百龄坛威士忌*流个不停
松树们一点一点进入我的胸口
秃山上
那些庞大沉闷的灰色巨石
也悄悄进入我的心
它们全都被喂饱了
鲜美的肥肉
和白乳酪爆米花
或者所有这些年来它们想吃的
无论什么东西

（孔亚雷　译）

* 百龄坛（Ballantine），始创于1827年的著名苏格兰威士忌品牌。

WHEN I DRINK

When I drink
the $300 scotch
with Roshi
it quenches every thirst
A song comes to my lips
a woman lies down with me
and every desire
invites me to curl up naked
in its dripping jaws

No more, I cry, no more
but Roshi fills my glass again
and new passions consume me
new appetites
For instance
I fall into a tulip
(and never hit the bottom)
or I hurtle through the night
in sweaty sexual union
with someone about twice the size
of the Big Dipper

When I eat meat with Roshi
the four-legged animals
don't cry any more
and the two-legged animals
don't try to fly away
and the exhausted salmon
come home to my hand
and Roshi's wolf
biting at its broken chain
creates a sensation
in the cabin
by making friends with everyone

When I chow down with Roshi
and the Ballantine flows
the pine trees inch into my bosom
the great boring grey boulders
of Mt. Baldy
creep into my heart
and they all get fed
with the delicious fat
and the white cheese popcorn
or whatever it is
they've wanted all these years

更好

比黑暗更好
是假黑暗
哄骗你
与某人的
古董的表亲
亲热

比银行更好
是假银行
你把所有暴利
兑换成
法币

比咖啡更好
是蓝咖啡
你喝它
在临终沐浴
要么等着
你的鞋
被脱去

比诗更好
是我的诗
它涉及
一切
美好与
尊严，而
又非矣

比野性更好

是秘密野性
如我在
停车场的
黑暗中
与新蛇一起

比艺术更好
是讨厌的艺术
它证明
比经文更好
衡量你进步的
微小尺度

比黑暗更好
是无暗
更黑更广
更深远
森然冻结
充满洞穴
和失明的隧道
那里出现
招手的已故亲人
和其他宗教
器皿

比爱更好
是禅爱
更细腻
超色情
小小静修者
巨大生殖器

13

却比思想更轻

安置于
迷雾眼睑里
顽强活着
从此后
做饭种花
生儿育女

比我母亲更好
是你母亲
她依然健在
而我的
已不在世
我在说什么！
原谅我，母亲

比我更好
是你
比我更善良
是你
更甜更灵更快
你你你
比我更美
比我更壮
比我更孤僻

我要
越来越好
了解你

——秃山，1996

（北岛　译）

14

BETTER

better than darkness
is fake darkness
which swindles you
into necking with
someone's antique
cousin

better than banks
are false banks
where you change
all your rough money
into legal tender

better than coffee
is blue coffee
which you drink
in your last bath
or sometimes waiting
for your shoes
to be dismantled

better than poetry
is my poetry
which refers
to everything
that is beautiful and
dignified, but is
neither of these itself

better than wild
is secretly wild
as when I am in
the darkness of
a parking space
with a new snake

better than art
is repulsive art
which demonstrates
better than scripture
the tiny measure
of your improvement

better than darkness
is darkless
which is inkier, vaster
more profound
and eerily refrigerated
filled with caves
and blinding tunnels
in which appear
beckoning dead relatives
and other religious
paraphernalia

better than love
is wuve
which is more refined
superbly erotic
tiny serene people
with huge genitalia
but lighter than thought
comfortably installed
on an eyelash of mist
and living grimly
ever after
cooking, gardening
and raising kids

better than my mother
is your mother
who is still alive
while mine
is not alive
but what am I saying!
forgive me mother

better than me
are you
kinder than me
are you

sweeter smarter faster
you you you
prettier than me
stronger than me
lonelier than me

I want to get
to know you
better and better

– Mt. Baldy, 1996

害相思病的和尚

我剃光了头
我穿上僧袍
我睡在一间小木屋的角落
在六千五百英尺的山上
这儿很凄凉
我惟一不需要的
就是梳子

——秃山，1997

THE LOVESICK MONK

I shaved my head
I put on robes
I sleep in the corner of a cabin
sixty-five hundred feet up a mountain
It's dismal here
The only thing I don't need
is a comb

– Mt. Baldy, 1997

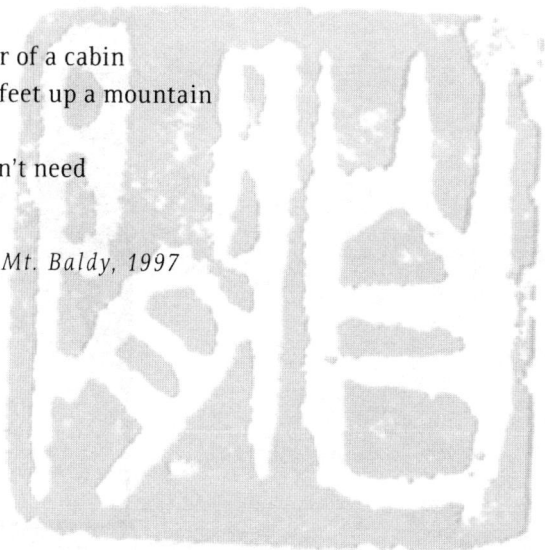

17

致一位年轻的尼姑

这无所求的爱
是我们交错的诞生
所赐予——
你有你的一代，
我有我的。
我不是
你要找的人。
你也不是
我已经放弃找的人。
时光如此甜蜜地
解决了我们
当我们手挽着手
走过细节之桥：
你切菜。
我烧饭。
你为爱而死。
我死而复生。

TO A YOUNG NUN

This undemanding love
that our staggered births
have purchased for us –
You in your generation,
I in mine.
I am not the one
you are looking for.
You are not the one
I've stopped looking for.
How sweetly time
disposes of us
as we go arm in arm
over the Bridge of Details:
Your turn to chop.
My turn to cook.
Your turn to die for love.
My turn to resurrect.

别的作家

史蒂夫·圣菲尔德是个了不起的俳
句大师。
他和莎拉，他美丽的妻子，
住在乡下，
他描写那些细小的事物
以表现所有事物。
佐佐木承周老师
曾让数百个和尚
彻底开悟，
他讲述宇宙
在同时
膨胀和收缩。
我写啊写
写一个高贵的年轻女人
在我的吉普车前座
解开她的牛仔裤
并让我触摸
生命的源头
因为我离它是如此之远。
我不得不告诉你，朋友们，
跟他们相比，
我更喜欢我写的东西。

OTHER WRITERS

Steve Sanfield is a great haiku master.
He lives in the country with Sarah,
his beautiful wife,
and he writes about the small things
which stand for all things.
Kyozan Joshu Roshi,
who has brought hundreds of monks
to a full awakening,
addresses the simultaneous
expansion and contraction
of the cosmos.
I go on and on
about a noble young woman
who unfastened her jeans
in the front seat of my jeep
and let me touch
the source of life
because I was so far from it.
I've got to tell you, friends,
I prefer my stuff to theirs.

老师

我从未真正听懂
他说的话
但时不时地
我发现自己
在跟狗一起叫
　　跟鸢尾花一起弯腰
或用其他的小方式
排忧解难

ROSHI

I never really understood
what he said
but every now and then
I find myself
barking with the dog
or bending with the irises
or helping out
in other little ways

药

我的药
有许多相反的口味。
沉迷于，或困惑于
它们之间的差别，
病人忘记了难受。

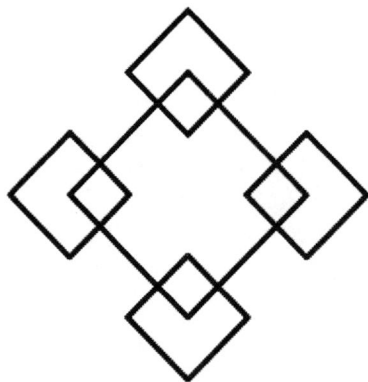

MEDICINE

My medicine
Has many contrasting flavours.
Engrossed in, or perplexed by
The differences between them,
The patient forgets to suffer.

真我

真我，真我
没有意志——
不存在"杀生"
或"不杀生"
但我
还是个见习僧
我全心全意地
奉行
第一条戒律
"不杀生"

TRUE SELF

True Self, True Self
has no will –
It's free from "Kill"
or "Do not kill"
but while I am
a novice still
I do embrace
with all my will
the First Commitment
"Do not kill"

老师

禅的崩溃

我可以把脸
塞进那个地方
跟我的呼吸搏斗
当她垂下热切的手指
　　打开自己，
好让我用整个嘴
解除她的饥渴，

　　她最隐秘的饥渴——
我何必还要开悟？
我是否错过了什么？
难道我已忘记昨天的蚊虫
或明天饥饿的幽灵？

我可以背一把刀在这山间漫游
只因喝多了拉图堡红酒*
我把我的心泼入
　　卡瓜斯**的光之山谷
当那条看门狗流着口水跳出灌木丛
并且不愿意认我
我吓得全身冰冷
然后我们就在那儿，没错，困惑不已
为谁该先杀了另一个——
我动它也动，
它动我也动，
我何必还要开悟？
我是否把什么留在了外面？
难道有某个世界我无法拥抱？
某根骨头我没有去偷？

耶稣如此爱我，以至于圣血

从他的心头滴落
我攀上一架铁梯
进入他胸膛的洞口
那是因为悲伤庞大如中国
我一袭白衣走进最深处的房间
我哀求我乞求
"不是这个，先生。也不是那个，
先生。求求你了，先生。"
我透过他的眼睛看去
无助的人们又被欺辱
人类温柔盛开的乳头
被强权、黑幕和金钱的
钳子夹住——
我何必还要寻求开悟？
难道我不认得那种蟑螂？
那种在我王陛下软泥中的害虫？

"男人愚蠢，女人发疯"
每个人都在圣胡安***和卡瓜斯沉睡
不醒
每个人都在爱 除了我
每个人都有信仰 有男友
有孤独的天赋——

可以运球穿越整个宇宙
我可以手也不动就让一个女人脱光
我为了小便而奔忙
　　把我高大的银色双肩
献给针头般的月亮——
我一如既往

24

为了某人转瞬即逝的美

而心碎

而一再谋划

但它们渐渐消失 如同没有书写的国度

现在，瞧，我一路呼哧呼哧

开往撒哈拉站

　　无与伦比的归隐

将空气搅入黑暗的

易忘之茧——

我何必在开悟的祭坛上瑟瑟发抖？

我何必要永远保持笑容？

THE COLLAPSE OF ZEN

When I can wedge my face
into the place
and struggle with my breathing
as she brings her eager fingers down
        to separate herself,
to help me use my whole mouth
against her hungriness,
        her most private of hungers –
why should I want to be enlightened?
Is there something that I missed?
Have I forgotten yesterday's mosquito
or tomorrow's hungry ghost?

When I can roam this hill with a knife in my back
caused by too much drinking of Chateau Latour
and spill my heart into the valley
        of the lights of Caguas
and freeze in fear as the watchdog
comes drooling out of the bushes
and refuses to recognize me
and there we are, yes, bewildered
as to who should kill the other first –
and I move and it moves,
and it moves and I move,
why should I want to be enlightened?
Did I leave something out?
Was there some world I failed to embrace?
Some bone I didn't steal?

When Jesus loves me so much that blood
        comes out of his heart
and I climb a metal ladder
into the hole in his bosom
which is caused by sorrow as big as China
and I enter the innermost room wearing white clothes

and I entreat and I plead:
"Not this one, Sir. Not that one, Sir. I beg you, Sir."
and I look through His eyes
as the helpless are shit on again
and the tender blooming nipple of mankind
is caught in the pincers
of power and muscle and money –
why should I seek enlightenment?
Did I fail to recognize some cockroach?
Some vermin in the ooze of my majesty?

When 'men are stupid and women are crazy'
and everyone is asleep in San Juan and Caguas
and everyone is in love but me
and everyone has a religion and a boyfriend
and a great genius for loneliness –

When I can dribble over all the universes
and undress a woman without touching her
and run errands for my urine
          and offer my huge silver shoulders
to the pinhead moon –
When my heart is broken as usual
over someone's evanescent beauty
and design after design
they fade like kingdoms with no writing
and, look, I wheeze my way
up to the station of Sahara's
          incomparable privacy
and churn the air into a dark cocoon
of effortless forgetting –
why should I shiver on the altar of enlightenment?
why should I want to smile forever?

秃山的清晨

闹钟凌晨2:30把我叫醒：
我穿上僧袍
和服和褶裙
式样仿自12世纪
弓术家的装束：
再外面是海青
一件厚重的外衣
袖子奇大无比：
再外面是挂络
一种碎布拼成的围兜
上面系着一块象牙色圆环：
最后是四英尺长
蛇一般蜿蜒的腰带
打成一个巨大漂亮的结
像块绞成辫形的哈拉面包
绑在挂络后面：
总共这些
大概20磅重的衣服
我在凌晨2:30
辉煌的勃起中
快速穿上

EARLY MORNING AT MT. BALDY

Alarm awakened me at 2:30 a.m.:
got into my robes
kimono and *hakama*
modelled after the 12th-century
archer's costume:
on top of this the *koroma*
a heavy outer garment
with impossibly large sleeves:
on top of this the *ruksu*
a kind of patchwork bib
which incorporates an ivory disc:
and finally the four-foot
serpentine belt
that twists into a huge handsome knot
resembling a braided *challah*
and covers the bottom of the *ruksu*:
all in all
about 20 pounds of clothing
which I put on quickly
at 2:30 a.m.
over my enormous hard-on

离开秃山

我下山了
经过多年的学习
和严格训练。
我把僧袍挂在
古老小屋的木钉上
在那儿我坐得多
睡得少。
我最终明白了
我不是修行
的料。
"谢谢你,亲爱的"
我听见心在喊
当我踏进圣莫尼卡高速的
车流,
西行洛杉矶。
许多人
(其中有些是习禅者)
开始问我一些关于"最高实在"*
的愤怒问题。
我想那是因为
他们不喜欢看见
老自闲抽烟。

——1999

LEAVING MT. BALDY

I came down from the mountain
after many years of study
and rigorous practice.
I left my robes hanging on a peg
in the old cabin
where I had sat so long
and slept so little.
I finally understood
I had no gift
for Spiritual Matters.
'Thank You, Beloved'
I heard a heart cry out
as I entered the stream of cars
on the Santa Monica Freeway,
westbound for L.A.
A number of people
(some of them practitioners)
have begun to ask me angry questions
about The Ultimate Reality.
I suppose it's because
they don't like to see
old Jikan smoking.

– 1999

---

* 最高实在(Ultimate Reality),禅宗术语,意思接近"终极真理"或"一切事物的主宰"。

Dear Roshi,
I'm sorry that I cannot
help you now, because
I met this woman.

Please forgive my
selfishness.

I send you
Birthday Greetings,
deep affection and
respect.

Jikan
the useless monk
bows his head

亲爱的老师:
　　很抱歉，现在我不能
　　服侍您了，因为
　　我遇见了这个女人。

　　请原谅我的
　　自私。

　　在此送上我的

生日祝福，
以及深深的爱和
敬意。

一个无用的弟子
自闲
垂首

30

世界上最幸运的男人

然后发生了很多事。我被一个无神论者在头上敲了一下。我一直没找回自信。即使到今天我还会被最微小的东西吓到。哈伯德老妈*搬进伤口并养了一窝孩子。多年来我的头都被绷带包着。我假装帮助每个人。

我清醒过来。我直面我的伤痛。松树出现了，灰色的群山，清晨远处雾蒙蒙的风景，人们过着有意思的生活。上帝，你的生活很有意思，我一直不停地说。我一直不停地在欢快的怀疑中摇头。

我有那么多话想对你说。我是世界上最幸运的男人。我学会了给兔子剥皮，留下很少的切口和很多的肘油。复活节是我的旺季。一刀下去它整个身体就从皮里滑出来，然后用可丽舒面巾纸把它塞满，卖掉。

礼拜六晚上的确是，就像他们说的，"一周中最孤独的晚上"。我盘腿而坐，旁边放着收音机和几个麻线球，说不定我想捆点什么。小木屋变得很冷，但我乐在其中。有时一只蜘蛛会吊着吓人的湿蛛丝垂下来，扰乱我来之不易的超然。

我的忠告十分有用。比如说，不要对着一个大松果撒尿。那也许不是一个松果。要是你搞不清哪种蜘蛛有毒，就把它们全干掉。长腿蜘蛛并非真正的蜘蛛：它其实属于'圣拉坦尼奥犯罪家族'。虽然虫子也珍惜生命，尽管它们不懈的勤奋是我们所有人的楷模，但它们很少有死的意识，就算它们有，也不会像你我那样，带着强烈的感情。生死对它们几乎是一回事。从这个意义上说，它们很像神秘主义者，而且像神秘主义者一样，很多都有毒。很难跟一只虫子做爱，特别是如果你的那个天生很大。就我个人的经验，没有一只虫子抱怨过。要是你不确定哪些神秘主义者有毒，那么最好见一个杀一个，用榔头给他头上来一下，或者用鞋，用大大的老蔬菜，比方说，一根巨大石化的日本萝卜。

——秃山，1997

---

* 《哈伯德老妈》（Old Mother Hubbard）是一首著名的英语童谣，讲的是哈伯德老妈和她养的小狗的故事。

The Luckiest Man in the World

Then a lot of things happened. I was struck on the head by an atheist. I never recovered my sense of confidence. Even today I am frightened by the smallest things. Old Mother Hubbard moved into the wound and produced her brood. For many years my head was laced up. I pretended to help everyone.

I sobered up. I faced my misery. Pine trees appeared, grey mountains, misty vistas in the early morning, people with interesting lives. G-d, your life is interesting, I never stopped saying. I never stopped shaking my head in convivial disbelief.

There's so much I want to tell you. I'm the luckiest man in the world. I learned to skin a rabbit with very few incisions and a lot of elbow grease. Easter is my big season. The whole thing comes off in one swoop and you stuff it with Kleenex and sell it.

Saturday night really is, as they say, 'the loneliest night of the week.' I hunker down with my radio and a few balls of twine, in case I want to tie something up. I let the cabin get very cold and I rejoice in my good fortune. Sometimes a spider will descend on its hideous wet thread and threaten my hard-earned disinterest.

My advice is highly valued. For instance, don't piss on a large pine cone. It may not be a pine cone. If you are not clear about which spiders are poisonous, kill them all. The daddy longlegs is not a true spider: it actually belongs to the Seratonio crime family. Although insects value their lives, and even though their relentless industry is an example for all of us, they rarely have a thought about death, and when they do, it is not accompanied by powerful emotions, as it is with you and me. They hardly discriminate between life and death. In this sense they are like mystics, and like mystics, many are poisonous. It is difficult to make love to an insect, especially if you are well endowed. As for my own experience, not one single insect has ever complained. If you are not sure which mystics are poisonous, it is best to kill the one you come across with a blow to the head using a hammer, or a shoe, or a large old vegetable, such as a petrified giant daikon radish.

– Mt. Baldy, 1997

曲终人散

大概十五岁的时候
我跟着一个漂亮女孩儿
加入了加拿大共产党。
那些秘密集会
如果你迟到一分钟
就会被大声呵斥。
我们研究傀儡们在华盛顿
通过的《麦卡伦法案》*
和傀儡的走狗们在被殖民的魁北克
通过的《派洛克法案》**；
他们对我们家
及我们家如何弄钱
说着令人作呕的屁话。
他们想推翻
这个我爱的国家
（我还在当兵，作为一名海童军）。
甚至那些
想改变现实的好人
他们也恨
并称其为社会法西斯。
他们计划对罪犯采取行动
比如我的那些舅舅和舅妈
甚至对我那可怜的小妈妈
他们也有计划

她当年逃出立陶宛
只带着两个冻苹果
和满满一头巾的大富翁纸币***。
他们从不让我接近那个女孩儿
那个女孩儿也从不让我接近那个
女孩儿。
她变得越来越漂亮
直到后来她嫁给一个律师
自己也成了社会法西斯
而且很可能也成了罪犯。
但我还是很崇拜共产党员
能为一些完全错误的东西
猪头猪脑地献身。
多年后我发现
自己也在干类似的事：
我加入了一个钢颚狂徒的小团伙
他们认为自己
是心灵世界的海军陆战队。
一切只是时间问题：
我们将用这条木筏登陆
到达彼岸。
我们将占领那片海滩
到达彼岸。

---

* 《麦卡伦法案》，又称《麦卡伦国内安全法》，1950年由美国国会通过，其目的在于镇压共产党并打击一切进步组织，因其由参议员麦卡伦提出而得名。
** 《派洛克法案》是1937年在加拿大魁北克通过的一个反动法案，其性质与《麦卡伦法案》类似。
*** 原文为monopoly money，指在大富翁游戏中使用的游戏纸币。

THE PARTY WAS OVER THEN TOO

When I was about fifteen
I followed a beautiful girl
into the Communist Party of Canada.
There were secret meetings
and you got yelled at
if you were a minute late.
We studied the McCarran Act
passed by the stooges in Washington
and the Padlock Law
passed by their lackeys in colonized Quebec;
and they said nasty shit
about my family
and how we got our money.
They wanted to overthrow
the country that I loved
(and served, as a Sea Scout).
And even the good people
who wanted to change things,
they hated them too
and called them social fascists.
They had plans for criminals
like my uncles and aunties
and they even had plans
for my poor little mother
who had slipped out of Lithuania
with two frozen apples
and a bandana full of monopoly money.
They never let me get near the girl
and the girl never let me get near the girl.
She became more and more beautiful
until she married a lawyer
and became a social fascist herself
and very likely a criminal too.
But I admired the Communists

for their pig-headed devotion
to something absolutely wrong.
It was years before I found
something comparable for myself:
I joined a tiny band of steel-jawed zealots
who considered themselves
the Marines of the spiritual world.
It's just a matter of time:
We'll be landing this raft
on the Other Shore.
We'll be taking that beach
on the Other Shore.

和尚头
艺术家的证据

就这样

就这样
我不会跟着你跑
我要休息半个钟头
就这样
我不会去舔
你的回忆
我不会再把脸在上面擦来擦去
我要打哈欠
我要伸懒腰
我要拿一根毛衣针
在鼻子上方
把脑袋戳穿
我的余生
都不想再爱你
我想让你的皮肤
从我的皮肤上脱落
我想用我的钳子
松开你的钳子
我不想再这样生活
伸着舌头
用又一首脏歌
代替
我的球棒

就这样
现在我要睡了，亲爱的
不要来拦我
我要睡了
我会一脸平和
我会睡得流口水
我会睡得很熟
不管你爱不爱我
就这样
新世界的秩序
皱纹和口臭
一切都将
跟从前不同
闭着眼睛
吃掉你
希望你不会醒来
就此离开
但那又是另外一回事
更糟的事
更蠢的事
诸如此类
只是更短

THIS IS IT

This is it
I'm not coming after you
I'm going to lie down for half an hour
This is it
I'm not going down
on your memory
I'm not rubbing my face in it any more
I'm going to yawn
I'm going to stretch
I'm going to put a knitting needle
up my nose
and poke out my brain
I don't want to love you
for the rest of my life
I want your skin
to fall off my skin
I want my clamp
to release your clamp
I don't want to live
with this tongue hanging out
and another filthy song
in the place
of my baseball bat

This is it
I'm going to sleep now darling
Don't try to stop me
I'm going to sleep
I'll have a smooth face
and I'm going to drool
I'll be asleep
whether you love me or not
This is it
The New World Order
of wrinkles and bad breath
It's not going to be
like it was before
eating you
with my eyes closed
hoping you won't get up
and go away
It's going to be something else
Something worse
Something sillier
Something like this
only shorter

这不是中国

抱紧我
告诉我世界像什么样
我不想往外看
我想靠你的眼睛
和嘴唇
我不想摸任何东西
除了老旧的保险杠上
你的手
我不想摸任何其他东西
要是你爱那些死石头
和粗糙的大松树
好吧那我也喜欢
告诉我风是不是
发出一种美丽的声音
我会闭上眼睛微笑
告诉我这是一个美好的早晨
还是一个晴朗的早晨
告诉我这是他妈的
什么样的早晨
我会买下来
然后让狗
别再鬼哭狼嚎
这不是中国
没有人吃它

好吧你要走就走
我会自己
创造出一个宇宙
我会让它们全都粘在我身上
每个忧郁的松果
每根无聊的松针
我会从这个光头里

360度地
广播慈爱
给所有壮丽的风景
给所有横越
明亮山峰的
雾与雪
给那些女人
她们在溪水中沐浴
在屋顶上梳头
给那些无声的人
他们用惊人的沉默
向我祈求
给那些心灵上的穷人
虽然他们很富有
给所有徒具思想外形
却裂了缝的精神
愿你从这里爬起
在幽灵般人生的尽头

– after a photo by Hazel Field

THIS ISN'T CHINA

Hold me close
and tell me what the world is like
I don't want to look outside
I want to depend on your eyes
and your lips
I don't want to feel anything
but your hand
on the old raw bumper
I don't want to feel anything else
If you love the dead rocks
and the huge rough pine trees
    Okay I like them too
Tell me if the wind
makes a pretty sound
I'll close my eyes and smile
Tell me if it's a good morning
or a clear morning
Tell me what the fuck
kind of morning it is
and I'll buy it
And get the dog
to stop whining and barking
This isn't China
nobody's going to eat it

    Okay go if you must

I'll create the cosmos
by myself
I'll let it all stick to me
every dismal pine cone
every boring pine needle
And I'll broadcast my affection
from this shaven dome
360 degrees
to all the dramatic vistas
to all the mists and snows
that move across
the shining mountains
to the women bathing
in the stream
and combing their hair
on the roofs
to the voiceless ones
who have petitioned me
from their surprising silence
to the poor in heart
though they be rich
to all the thought-forms
and leaking mental objects
that you get up here
at the end of your ghostly life

高轮王子酒店吧

滑入极乐世界
滑入清醒的醉国
滑入熔炉惟一惟一惟一亲爱真主安拉的
蓝色之心
危险情绪的伴侣——
滑入我自己宗教的
27个地狱我自己那甜蜜
黑暗的醉教
我跪下的诗歌之膝我的僧袍
我的托钵我的诗歌之鞭
我最后的割礼之前
是肉体的割礼
心灵的割礼
渴望的割礼
为了回归为了被救赎
为了被清洗为了被再一次原谅
这最后的割礼这最后的
伟大的割礼——
被瞬间击垮
在可怕开悟的
爆炸光芒中
胆怯不已
但最后终于向放弃诗歌的伟大
投降
这并非某种聪明的经验
或者竞争意识那虚伪的
吻，而是我自己那甜蜜黑暗的
诗歌宗教我的蠢才奖
我的凉鞋和我可耻的祈祷
我那看不见的墨西哥蜡烛

我那没用的油脂
拿来清洁房屋并消除情敌
对我女朋友记忆所下的咒语——
哦诗歌我最后的割礼：
所有痛苦都在于害怕
和漠视那个少女的声音
那个少女的触摸和那个少女
芬芳而谦卑的妩媚
三次大战前它们就已消失——
哦我的爱我又爱上了你
我是你的狗你的猫
你的克娄巴特拉蛇*
为这最后的无形割礼
我毫无痛苦地流血
当我把你的衣裳撩起一点
亲吻你那奇迹般
分泌乳汁的膝盖
所有你们这些围观的人
上帝不容！
当我滑入爱中
愿你们受苦受难——
愿你们飞快地被
自己黑暗少女宗教
的妩媚
所包围

"以让你想起我的方式崇拜我"
她说："现在你相信我了？"
我自己黑暗少女宗教的妩媚

---

* 克娄巴特拉（Cleopatra），人称"埃及艳后"，古埃及的最后一任法老，传说她为保
护国家免受罗马帝国吞并，色诱了恺撒大帝及其手下，最后自杀身亡——方法是故意
让一条毒蛇咬死自己。

TAKANAWA PRINCE HOTEL BAR

Slipping down into the Pure Land
into the Awakened State of Drunk
into the furnace blue Heart of the
one one one true Allah the Beloved
Companion of Dangerous Moods –
Slipping down into the 27 Hells
of my own religion my own sweet
dark religion of drunk religion
my bended knee of Poetry my robes
my bowl my scourge of Poetry
my final circumcision after
the circumcision of the flesh
and the circumcision of the heart
and the circumcision of the yearning
to Return to be Redeemed
to be Washed to be Forgiven Again
the Final Circumcision the Final
and Great Circumcision –
Broken down awhile
and cowarding
in the blasting rays
of Hideous Enlightenment
but now finally surrendered to the Great
Resignation of Poetry
and not the kind of Wise Experience
or the false kisses of Competitive
Insight, but my own sweet dark
religion of Poetry my booby prize
my sandals and my shameful prayer
my invisible Mexican candle
my useless oils to clean the house
and remove my rival's spell
on my girlfriend's memory –

O Poetry my Final Circumcision:
All the pain was in fearing
and ignoring the girl's voice
and the girl's touch and the girl's
fragrant humbling girlishness
which was lost three wars ago –
And O my love I love you again
I am your dog your cat
your Cleopatran snake
I am bleeding painlessly
from the Final Formless Circumcision
as I push up your dress a little way
and kiss your miraculously
lactating knee
And may all of you who watch
and G-d forbid!
are in a suffering predicament
as I go sliding down to Love –
may you speedily be embraced by
the girlishness of your own
dark girlish religion

清泉在跳舞

清泉的身体修长。
她的光头
威胁着天窗
她的脚踩到
苹果地窖。
当她在千载难逢的
庆典上
为我们跳舞,
大餐厅里,
一堆轻飘飘的和尚
和尼姑,
就像个呼啦圈
绕着她的臀部飞转。
庄重古老的松林
抛开卫兵的职责
加入了狂欢,
圣加百利山也来了
还有克莱蒙,阿普兰
以及内陆帝国*的
那些平原城市。
海洋跟海洋对话
说,见鬼了,
我们也上,我们自己动起来。
银河卸下它的轮轴
紧紧黏住先生的腰,
还有那遥远的宇宙,
和未来世界,
更别说那些孕育着反物质的
深邃黑洞,
而像这首诗一样
天马行空的思绪,
破坏了整个气氛。
一切都在围着她的臀部,
及她臀部包裹的东西旋转;

一切都被她的面孔，
她那无主的表情照亮。
然后有个痛苦的傻蛋
在这儿，不，这儿
他以为
清泉还是个女人，
还想找个立足之地
在清泉不跳舞的地方。

---

* 内陆帝国（Inland Empire），南加州一个区域的简称，以河滨市和圣博娜迪诺市为中心。

SEISEN IS DANCING

Seisen has a long body.
Her shaved head
threatens the skylight
and her feet go down
into the apple cellar.
When she dances for us
at one of our infrequent
celebrations,
the dining hall,
with its cargo of weightless monks
and nuns,
bounces around her hips
like a Hula Hoop.
The venerable old pine trees
crack out of sentry duty
and get involved,
as do the San Gabriel Mountains
and the flat cities
of Claremont, Upland
and the Inland Empire.
Ocean speaks to ocean
saying, What the hell,
let's go with it, rouse ourselves.
The Milky Way undoes its spokes
and cleaves to Seisen's haunches,
as do the worlds beyond,
and worlds unborn,
not to mention darkest holes
of brooding anti-matter,
and random flying mental objects
like this poem,
fucking up the atmosphere.
It's all going round her hips,
and what her hips enclose;
it's all lit up by her face,
her ownerless expression.
And then there's this aching fool
over here, no, over here
who thinks that
Seisen's still a woman,
who's trying to find a place to stand
where Seisen isn't Dancing.

进入一个阶段

我们正在进入一个迷茫的阶段，一个奇妙的时刻，人们在绝望中发现了光亮，又在希望的巅峰感到晕眩。这也是一个宗教的时刻，而这正是危险所在。人们想要听从权威的声音，而光是何为权威每个脑袋里都会涌出许多怪异的想法。家庭重新以基石的面目出现，更受敬重，更受赞扬，但我们中间那些曾被另外可能性刺穿过的人，只会越过那些潮流，即使那是爱的潮流。公众对秩序的渴求只会招来许多顽固不化分子的强加于人。动物园的悲哀将落到社会身上。

你和我，渴望无罪的亲密，我们会连充满好奇的第一个字也不愿说起，因为怕报复。每一个绝望都藏在一个玩笑背后。但我发誓我将呆在你的香水范围之内。

今晚的月亮看上去多么严厉，就像一位铁处女的面孔，而非平常那模糊的白痴。

如果你觉得弗洛伊德现在已经被玷辱，还有爱因斯坦，海明威，那么就等着瞧，跟在我后面来的那些家伙，会对这帮白头发做些什么。

但还是将会有一个十字架，一个标志，有些人会明白；一次秘密会面，一句警告，一个藏在耶路撒冷的耶路撒冷。我将穿上白衣，一如往常，我将走进内心最深处，正如我一代一代曾经做过的那样，去乞求，去申诉，去辩解。我将走进新娘和新郎的洞房，没有人会跟着我。

毫无疑问，在不久的将来，从像我这样的人那里，我们将会看到和听到更多这一类的事情。

MOVING INTO A PERIOD

We are moving into a period of bewilderment, a curious moment in which people find light in the midst of despair, and vertigo at the summit of their hopes. It is a religious moment also, and here is the danger. People will want to obey the voice of Authority, and many strange constructs of just what Authority is will arise in every mind. The family will appear again as the Foundation, much honoured, much praised, but those of us who have been pierced by other possibilities, we will merely go through the motions, albeit the motions of love. The public yearning for Order will invite many stubborn uncompromising persons to impose it. The sadness of the zoo will fall upon society.

You and I, who yearn for blameless intimacy, we will be unwilling to speak even the first words of inquisitive delight, for fear of reprisals. Everything desperate will live behind a joke. But I swear that I will stand within the range of your perfume.

How severe seems the moon tonight, like the face of an Iron Maiden, instead of the usual indistinct idiot.

If you think Freud is dishonoured now, and Einstein, and Hemingway, just wait and see what is to be done with all that white hair, by those who come after me.

But there will be a Cross, a sign, that some will understand; a secret meeting, a warning, a Jerusalem hidden in Jerusalem. I will be wearing white clothes, as usual, and I will enter The Innermost Place as I have done generation upon generation, to entreat, to plead, to justify. I will enter the chamber of the Bride and the Bridegroom, and no one will follow me.

Have no doubt, in the near future we will be seeing and hearing much more of this sort of thing from people like myself.

我一直没找到那个女孩
我一直没发财
跟我学

2003年9月

just to
have been
one of them

even
on the
lowest
rung

לאל ברוך נעימות יתנו

只要曾是他们中的一员
哪怕在最低一级

我的王妃

有这么一个庞大的女人，
（哦，老天，她真美）
这庞大的女人，
尽管她是所有女人，
却有非常独特的个性；
这庞大的女人
有时会在很早的清晨
来找我
并让我欲仙欲死！
在松树林好几英里之上
我们"在天堂四处翻滚"
我们亲密无间，
但我们并非双位一体
或那之类的玩意儿。
我们是两个巨人，
两具宏伟的身躯
充满柔情蜜意，
所有欢乐都被感受被放大
以符合我们的尺寸。
每当如此
我通常都乐于原谅每个
不够爱我的人
包括你，撒哈拉，
尤其是你。

My Consort

There is this huge woman,
(O G-d she's beautiful)
this huge woman
who, even though she is all women,
has a very specific character;
this huge woman
who sometimes comes to me
very early in the morning
and plucks me out of my skin!
We 'roll around heaven'
several miles above the pine trees
and there's no space between us,
but we're not One
or anything like that.
We're two huge people,
two immense bodies
of tenderness and delight,
with all the pleasures felt and magnified
to match our size.
Whenever this happens
I am usually ready to forgive everyone
who doesn't love me enough
including you, Sahara,
especially you.

历史悠久的克莱蒙村

我不记得
点过这支烟
我也不记得
我是一个人
还是在等谁。
我不记得何曾
见过这么多
漂亮的男人女人
在历史悠久的克莱蒙村
走来走去。
我一定锻炼过
因为我不记得
我怎么有这些肌肉;
还有这安详的表情:
我一定花了很多时间
思考那些垃圾事情。
孩子们经过我的长椅
被很快拉走
但年轻人
对他们秘密墓园里
这不寻常的庞然大物
的命运
深感兴趣,
他们转过身

回头看我。
长椅说,
"你要被风吹走了。"
钱包说,
"你六十二了。"
七层楼高的
尼桑探路者*说,
"请把你的钥匙
插进方向盘后面
那个银色的地方。
那叫点火开关。"

——1997年3月2日

---

*尼桑探路者(Nissan Pathfinder),一款运动型多功能越野车。

HISTORIC CLAREMONT VILLAGE

I don't remember
lighting this cigarette
and I don't remember
if I'm here alone
or waiting for someone.
I don't remember when
I've ever seen so many
beautiful men and women
walking back and forth
in Historic Claremont Village.
I must have been working out
because I don't remember
how I got these muscles;
and this serene expression:
I must have done my time
reflecting on the bullshit.
Children are pulled quickly
past my bench
but the young are deeply

interested
in the fate
of this unusually bulky presence
in their secret cemeteries,
and they twist around
to look back at me.
The bench says,
"You're going to blow away."
The wallet says,
"You're sixty-two."
The seven-storey
Nissan Pathfinder says,
"Try to put your key
in that silver place behind
the steering wheel.
It's called the ignition."

– March 2, 1997

心乱之晨

啊。那。
那就是我这个早晨
如此心乱的原因:
我的欲望回来了,
我再一次想要你。
我做得很好,
我超然面对一切。
男孩和女孩们都很美丽
而我是个老人,爱着每个人。
但现在我再一次想要你,
想要你全部的注意,
想要你的内裤迅速滑落
还挂在一只脚上,
而我脑海一片空白
只想着要到
那惟一的里面
那里
没有里,
也没有外。

DISTURBED THIS MORNING

Ah. That.
That's what I was so disturbed
about this morning:
my desire has come back,
and I want you again.
I was doing so fine,
I was above it all.
The boys and girls were beautiful
and I was an old man, loving everyone.
And now I want you again,
I want your absolute attention,
your underwear rolled down in a hurry
still hanging on one foot,
and nothing on my mind
but to be inside
the only place
that has
no inside,
and no outside.

寂寞之躯

她用她的脚进入我的脚
她用她的雪进入我的腰。
她进入我的心说，
"对，就这样。"
于是这寂寞之躯
从外面被覆盖，
从里面
被拥抱。
现在每当我想要吸气
她就会对着我的屏息低语，
"对，我的爱，就这样，就这样。"

BODY OF LONELINESS

She entered my foot with her foot
and she entered my waist with her snow.
She entered my heart saying,
"Yes, that's right."
And so the Body of Loneliness
was covered from without,
and from within
the Body of Loneliness was embraced.
Now every time I try to draw a breath
she whispers to my breathlessness,
"Yes, my love, that's right, that's right."

the face
can be
composed
so as to
never
appear
foolish
but rather
menacingly
unbalanced

脸可以被画得看上去一点都不蠢
但却不平衡得吓人

（孔亚雷　译）

我的所有消息

1
我本不会
出人头地
在当今
这市镇

而将来
有人会找
有用的
改变思路

从屠杀
以和平之名
到光荣的
复杂，

从而影响
政治
以更深入的
审核。

人们不会
再怕
在这条道
成交。

2
俯视
仰望，
用爱的

非人眼睛

相对的
感情
（破碎的心
治愈的病），

而带来
每个转机
领导下跪
才学会。

那厌恶沉重
思想的人
会珍视
并折好小床。

3
别解读
我的哭喊——
那是道
非名。

不要解构
我无药的高潮
我清醒但
喜欢飞翔。

紧跟上
我开放的言说，

你不必撬开
古老的锁。

4
神秘此刻，
此刻昭然
我屈于汝
心悦诚服。

我悄声低语
深怀感激
为心潮起伏的
每滴泪；

谁让我穿越
时间之墙
我可以触摸
每位来者

用我父母

说出的智慧
（基于一个
传闻），

未诞生想法
的速记
与优雅努力
合在一起。

5
无法破译
就让我的歌
重新接好
错误电路，

用你脑中
我的打油诗，
让那桥
再次拱起。

（北岛　译）

61

ALL MY NEWS

1.

I was not meant
to be renown
in the present
market town,

but in the future
some may find
what might be used
to change a mind

from slaughter
in the name of peace
to honouring
complexities,

and thus influence
politics
with deeper balance
deeper checks.

And no one has
to be afraid
when on this Path
the deal is made.

2.

Look on low
look on high,
see with Love's
inhuman eye

not only charge
of opposites
(the broken heart
the healing fix),

but what engenders
every turn –
the leader on her
knees will learn.

And he who's sick
with heavy thought
will cherish it
and fold his cot.

3.

Do not decode
these cries of mine –
They are the road,
and not the sign.

Nor deconstruct
my drugless high –
I'm sober but
I like to fly.

Then quickened with
my open talk,
you need not pick
the ancient lock.

4.

Mystery now,
and now Revealed
I bend to Thee
my will to yield,

and whisper here
my gratitude
for every tear
of restless mood;

Who let me breach
the walls of time
so I could touch
the ones to come

with wisdom that
my parents spoke
(established on an
anecdote),

and shorthand of
the unborn mind
with Graceful effort

all combined.

5.
Undeciphered
let my song
rewire circuits
wired wrong,

and with my jingle
in your brain,
allow the Bridge
to arch again.

你是对的，撒哈拉

你是对的，撒哈拉。没有迷雾，面纱，或者远方。迷雾被迷雾笼罩；面纱被面纱遮盖；而远方不断被远方拉远。那就是为什么没有迷雾，面纱，或者远方。那就是为什么这儿被称为"远离雾纱之地"。在这儿，旅行者变成了流浪者，流浪者变成了迷失者，迷失者变成了探寻者，探寻者变成了热恋者，热恋者变成了叫花子，叫花子变成了可怜虫，可怜虫变成了必须被牺牲的人，必须被牺牲的人变成了涅槃者，涅槃者又变成了超越者。一千年，或者一下午，一个人就这样在轮回的烈焰中旋转，历经所有变形，一个接一个，结束又开始，开始又结束，一秒钟86 000次。然后这个人，如果是男人，将会爱上撒哈拉这个女人；而这个人，如果是女人，将会爱上那个歌唱"远离雾纱之地"的男人。那个在等待的人是你吗，撒哈拉，还是我？

YOU ARE RIGHT, SAHARA

You are right, Sahara. There are no mists, or veils, or distances. But the mist is surrounded by a mist; and the veil is hidden behind a veil; and the distance continually draws away from the distance. That is why there are no mists, or veils, or distances. That is why it is called The Great Distance of Mist and Veils. It is here that The Traveller becomes The Wanderer, and The Wanderer becomes The One Who Is Lost, and The One Who Is Lost becomes The Seeker, and The Seeker becomes The Passionate Lover, and The Passionate Lover becomes The Beggar, and The Beggar becomes The Wretch, and The Wretch becomes The One Who Must Be Sacrificed, and The One Who Must Be Sacrificed becomes The Resurrected One, and The Resurrected One becomes The One Who Has Transcended The Great Distance of Mist and Veils. Then for a thousand years, or the rest of the afternoon, such a One spins in the Blazing Fire of Changes, embodying all the transformations, one after the other, and then beginning again, and then ending again, 86,000 times a second. Then such a One, if he is a man, is ready to love the woman Sahara; and such a One, if she is a woman, is ready to love the man who can put into song The Great Distance of Mist and Veils. Is it you who is waiting, Sahara, or is it me?

初级问题

为什么庵堂里那些容光焕发的尼姑在学习你的著作，而我却在寒风呼啸的冬天一个人呆在小木屋，喝着名叫"滑溜"的茶？

为什么你高高在上，做着一场关于万物起源的晦涩布道，其中包括一些有关男女契约的可疑言论，而我却在地板上扭成莲花坐（这可真不是北美人能做的），用网格线比划着闪亮的现代都市，那儿远离你的掌管，民主和浪漫能够繁荣昌盛？

为什么当我为了让你熟悉我们的文化，放重要的黄色录像给你看，你却睡着了？为什么当它们放完了，你又突然醒过来说："研究人类的爱很有意思，但也不是那么有意思"？

为什么"大乘"*，它能在古色古香的京都街道上跑得那么欢快，却不能适应秃山的之字形山道？如果它不能，那它对我们有什么用？

为什么鸢尾花对你弯腰，而危险的松果却从那么高的地方掉到我们没有保护的光头？

为什么你命令我们讲，然后却又自己讲？

那是因为一阵钟声把我唤到你的房间，那是因为我在伴你左右的荣幸中无言以对，那是因为我在某种无法形容的亲切所散发的芬芳中踉踉跄跄，那是因为我已经忘了所有的问题，我一头摔倒在地，消失在你之中。

——秃山，1998

---

*原文为Great Vehicle，大乘佛法的英译，这里将其比喻成某种车辆。

EARLY QUESTIONS

Why do cloisters of radiant nuns study your production, while I drink the tea called Smooth Move, alone in my cabin during the howling winter?

Why do you mount the High Seat and deliver an incomprehensible discourse on The Source of All Things, which includes questionable observations on the contract between men and women, while I sit on the floor twisted into the Lotus Position (which is not meant for North Americans), laying out the grid-lines of shining modern cities where, far from your authority, democracy and romance can flourish?

Why do you fall asleep when, in order to familiarize you with our culture, I screen important sex videos, and then when they're finished, why do you suddenly wake up and say: "Study human love interesting, but not so interesting?"

Why can't the Great Vehicle, which rolls so merrily through the quaint streets of Kyoto, make it up the switchbacks of Mt. Baldy? And if it can't, is it any good to us?

Why do the irises bend to you, while dangerous pine cones fall from a considerable height on our unprotected bald heads?

Why do you command us to talk, and then talk instead?

It is because a bell has summoned me to your room, it is because I am speechless in the honour of your company, it is because I am reeling in the fragrance of some unutterable hospitality, it is because I have forgotten all my questions, that I throw myself to the floor, and vanish into yours.

– Mt. Baldy, 1998

月亮

月亮在外面。
刚才我去小便的时候
看见了这个伟大而简洁的东西。
我应该看得再久一点。
我是个可怜的月亮爱好者。
我突然就看见了它
对我和月亮
都是这样。

THE MOON

The moon is outside.
I saw the great uncomplicated thing
when I went to take a leak just now.
I should have looked at it longer.
I am a poor lover of the moon.
I see it all at once and that's it
for me and the moon.

甜蜜时光

时光感觉多么甜蜜
当一切都太晚

当你不必再跟随
她摇曳的臀部

一路进入
你饥渴的想象

SWEET TIME

How sweet time feels
when it's too late

and you don't have to follow
her swinging hips

all the way into
your dying imagination

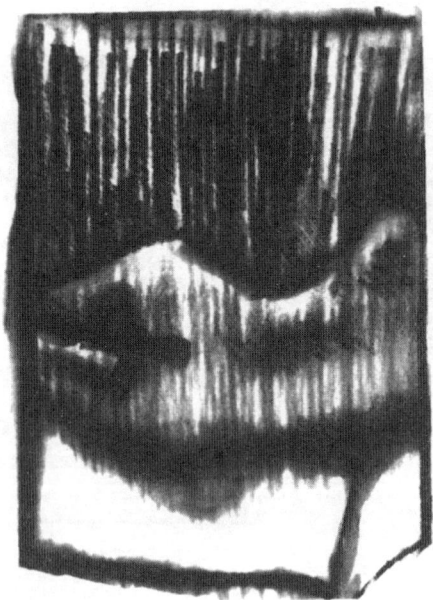

味道不错

味道不错
但我宁愿不吃
这尘世间
触摸一个美丽的少女
是莫大荣幸
但原谅我
如果我弃之而去
或改天再来
冥想能平静焦躁的心
广告大概是这么说
但它却让我
一头撞上墙
闲言碎语 气喘吁吁
再说
我并不想跟每个人都做朋友
我没那么多时间
我在断食
我在秘密地断食
让脸变瘦
那么上帝就能像以前
那样爱我
对其他的事
我毫无兴趣

FOOD TASTES GOOD

Food tastes good
but I'd rather not eat
Touching a beautiful young woman
is a great honour
in this vale of tears
forgive me if I pass on this
or take a rain check
Meditation calms the fevered heart
or so the advertising goes
but it drives me
up the wall
of gossip and breathlessness
Furthermore
I don't want to be a friend to everyone
I haven't got that much time
I'm fasting
I'm fasting secretly
to make my face thin
so G-d can love me
as He did before
I had the slightest interest
in these matters

好玩

信上帝
真的很好玩
什么时候你一定要试试
现在就试
看看上帝
是不是
想让你
信他

FUN

It is so much fun
to believe in G-d
You must try it sometime
Try it now
and find out whether
or not
G-d wants you
to believe in Him

we are not
convinced
there has
been any
improvement

我们无法相信有过什么进步

篮子

你应该走遍
所有地方
找回那些
为你而写的诗，
你可以在上面签下你的名字。
不要跟任何人
讨论这些事。
找啊。找啊。
当篮子满了
有人会出现
你可以把篮子交给她。
她会摊开她宽大的裙子
在一块黑石头上
坐下
然后在她腿上的
无限风光里
你的篮子会弹起来
像阳光下的一个斑点。

BASKET

You should go
from place to place
recovering the poems
that have been written for you,
to which you can affix your signature.
Don't discuss these matters
with anyone.
Retrieve. Retrieve.
When the basket is full
someone will appear
to whom you can present it.
She will spread her wide skirt
and sit down
on a black stone
and your basket will bounce
like a speck in sunlight
on the immense landscape
of her lap.

I believe that
you are standing
in the place
where I am
supposed to be
standing

Montreal
2003

我相信你正站在我应该站的地方
蒙特利尔 2003

（孔亚雷 译）

73

河流黑暗处

河流黑暗处
我辗转徘徊
我度过一生
在巴比伦

我忘记了
我的圣歌
我无能为力
在巴比伦

河流黑暗处
我无从看见
等在那儿的人
狩猎我的人

他切开我的唇
切开我的心
因而我无法
畅饮河流黑暗

他覆盖了我
我从中看到
我的非法的心
我的婚戒

我不知道
我无从看到
等在那儿的人
狩猎我的人

河流黑暗处
我惊慌失措
我最终属于
巴比伦

他用致命一击
刺穿我的心
他说："这心
不是你的。"

他把我的婚戒
交给了风
让我与万物
旋转不停

河流黑暗处
受伤的黎明中
我度过一生
在巴比伦

我从枯枝
获取我的歌
歌与树
为他高唱

未说出的真理
消逝的祝福
如果忘记
我的巴比伦

我不知道　　　　　河流黑暗处
我无从看见　　　　清凉世界
等在那儿的人　　　河流黑暗处
狩猎我的人　　　　在巴比伦

（北岛　译）

BY THE RIVERS DARK

By the rivers dark
I wandered on
I lived my life
in Babylon

and I did forget
my holy song
and I had no strength
in Babylon

by the rivers dark
where I could not see
who was waiting there
who was hunting me

and he cut my lip
and he cut my heart
so I could not drink
from the river dark

and he covered me
and I saw within
my lawless heart
and my wedding ring

I did not know
and I could not see
who was waiting there
who was hunting me

by the rivers dark
I panicked on
I belonged at last
to Babylon

then he struck my heart
with a deadly force
and he said, "This heart
it is not yours."

and he gave the wind
my wedding ring
and he circled me
with everything

by the rivers dark
in a wounded dawn
I live my life
in Babylon

tho' I take my song
from a withered limb
both song and tree
they sing for him

be the truth unsaid
and the blessing gone
if I forget
my Babylon

I did not know
and I could not see
who was waiting there
who was hunting me

by the rivers dark
where it all goes on
by the rivers dark
in Babylon

爱

给L.W.

光线穿过窗户，
直接来自上面的太阳，
于是我小小的房间
充满了爱的光芒。

在光流中我清楚地看见
平常你很少看见的灰尘，
从中无名者
让像我这样的人出了名。

我将试着再多说一点：
爱不停地走啊走
直到碰到一扇开着的门——
爱自己就不见了。

阳光下一切纷纷扰扰
微尘在漂浮在起舞，
我跟着它们一起忙乱
陷入虚无缥缈

于是我从去的地方回来
我的房间，它看上去一模一样——
但在无名和有名之间
什么都没剩下。

我将试着再多说一点：
爱不停地走啊走
直到碰到一扇开着的门——
爱自己就不见了。

LOVE ITSELF

for L.W.

The light came through the window,
Straight from the sun above,
And so inside my little room
There plunged the rays of Love.

In streams of light I clearly saw
The dust you seldom see,
Out of which the Nameless makes
A Name for one like me.

I'll try to say a little more:
Love went on and on
Until it reached an open door –
Then Love Itself was gone.

All busy in the sunlight
The flecks did float and dance,
And I was tumbled up with them
In formless circumstance.

Then I came back from where I'd been
My room, it looked the same –
But there was nothing left between
The Nameless and the Name.

I'll try to say a little more:
Love went on and on
Until it reached an open door –
Then Love Itself was gone.

你已经爱够了

我说我要做你的爱人。
你笑我说的话。
我永远地失业了。
我被当成一个死人。

我打扫大理石房间，
你却把我赶到下面。
你不让我相信
直到你让我明白：

我不是那个在爱的人——
是爱抓住了我。
当厌恶带着他的包裹出现，
你不准他投递。

当想被你抚摸的饥渴
从饥渴里升起，
你低声说，"你已经爱够了，
现在让我做你的爱人。"

YOU HAVE LOVED ENOUGH

I said I'd be your lover.
You laughed at what I said.
I lost my job forever.
I was counted with the dead.

I swept the marble chambers,
But you sent me down below.
You kept me from believing
Until you let me know:

That I am not the one who loves –
It's love that seizes me.
When hatred with his package comes,
You forbid delivery.

And when the hunger for your touch
Rises from the hunger,
You whisper, "You have loved enough,
Now let me be the Lover."

一千个吻那么深
给桑蒂1945—1998

1.
清晨你来到我身边
像触摸一块肉那样触摸我
你必须是个男人才会明白
那感觉多么甜蜜，多么美妙
我的镜中人我的至亲
我在睡梦中也认得你
除了你没人会将我收留
一千个吻那么深

我爱你，当你像朵百合
向着炎热盛开
而我是另一个雪人
伫立在雨雪之中
用他冰冻的爱
和二手身体去爱你
用他现在和曾经的全部
一千个吻那么深

我知道你不得不撒谎
我知道你不得不欺骗
为了透过哄骗的面纱
装得无比性感和骄傲
我们完美的色情贵族
如此优雅而低俗
我老了，但我依然陷入
一千个吻那么深

而我还在和酒一起工作
还在脸贴着脸跳舞

乐队在演奏《友谊万岁》
我的心不会退缩
我和迪吉及但丁一起混
我从未有他们那样威风
但偶尔他们也会让我露两手
一千个吻那么深

秋天掠过你的肌肤
有什么进入我的眼睛
一道无需存在
也无需消失的光
一个爱之书里的谜
晦涩而陈腐
直到在时间与鲜血中它又被见证
一千个吻那么深

我擅长爱也擅长恨
这之间我不知所措
我在练习但已经太晚
已经晚了太久
不过你看上去不错，真的不错

不羁街的骄傲
定有人为你神魂颠倒
一千个吻那么深

我爱你，当你像朵百合
向着炎热盛开
而我是另一个雪人
伫立在雨雪之中
但现在你已无需再听
而且我说的每句话
都让你厌恶
一千个吻那么深。

2.
小马疾奔，女孩儿青春
机会就在前方
你赢了一阵，接着便结束了
小小的连胜
现在你被召去
对付你那无敌的失败
你活得好像，人生非梦
一千个吻那么深

我玩手段我又出山
我回到不羁街
我失去把握，脚底一滑
掉进了一部杰作

也许我还有许多路要走
还有承诺要守*
我抛弃所有，但求活命
一千个吻那么深

在性的约束里，我们探求着
海的极限
我发现已经没有海洋
留给我这样的拾荒者
我费力走上前甲板
为我们残余的舰队祝福
然后同意被击沉
一千个吻那么深

我玩手段我又出山
我回到不羁街
我猜他们不会换走
属于你的礼物
有时，当长夜漫漫
我们这些不幸柔弱的人
会收拾好心前行
一千个吻那么深

对你的想念散发着芬芳
你的档案已经完整
除了我们忘做的那些
一千个吻那么深

---

*这句诗可能典出于美国诗人罗伯特·弗罗斯特（Robert Frost）一首著名的小诗《雪夜伫立林边》（Stopping by Wood on a Snowy Evening），诗的最后一段是：林子可爱，又黑又深，/但我还有承诺要守，/睡前还有许多路要走，/睡前还有许多路要走。（The woods are lovely, dark and deep, /But I have promises to keep, /And miles to go before I sleep, / And miles to go before I sleep.）

THOUSAND KISSES DEEP

for Sandy 1945–1998

1.

You came to me this morning
And you handled me like meat
You'd have to be a man to know
How good that feels how sweet
My mirror twin my next of kin
I'd know you in my sleep
And who but you would take me in
A thousand kisses deep

I loved you when you opened
Like a lily to the heat
I'm just another snowman
Standing in the rain and sleet
Who loved you with his frozen love
His second-hand physique
With all he is and all he was
A thousand kisses deep

I know you had to lie to me
I know you had to cheat
To pose all hot and high behind
The veils of sheer deceit
Our perfect porn aristocrat
So elegant and cheap
I'm old but I'm still into that
A thousand kisses deep

And I'm still working with the wine
Still dancing cheek to cheek
The band is playing Auld Lang Syne
The heart will not retreat
I ran with Diz and Danté

I never had their sweep
But once or twice they let me play
A thousand kisses deep
The autumn slipped across your skin
Got something in my eye
A light that doesn't need to live
And doesn't need to die
A riddle in the book of love
Obscure and obsolete
Till witnessed here in time and blood
A thousand kisses deep

I'm good at love I'm good at hate
It's in between I freeze
Been working out but it's too late
It's been too late for years
But you look fine you really do
The pride of Boogie Street
Somebody must have died for you
A thousand kisses deep

I loved you when you opened
Like a lily to the heat
I'm just another snowman
Standing in the rain and sleet
But you don't need to hear me now
And every word I speak
It counts against me anyhow
A thousand kisses deep.

2.

The ponies run the girls are young
The odds are there to beat

You win a while and then it's done
Your little winning streak
And summoned now to deal
With your invincible defeat
You live your life as if it's real
A thousand kisses deep.

I'm turning tricks I'm getting fixed
I'm back on Boogie Street
You lose your grip and then you slip
Into the Masterpiece
And maybe I had miles to drive
And promises to keep
You ditch it all to stay alive
A thousand kisses deep

Confined to sex we pressed against
The limits of the sea
I saw there were no oceans left

For scavengers like me
I made it to the forward deck
I blessed our remnant fleet
And then consented to be wrecked
A thousand kisses deep
I'm turning tricks, I'm getting fixed
I'm back on Boogie Street
I guess they won't exchange the gifts
That you were meant to keep
And sometimes when the night is slow
The wretched and the meek
We gather up our hearts and go
A thousand kisses deep

And fragrant is the thought of you
The file on you complete
Except what we forgot to do
A thousand kisses deep

分

我该怎么办
对这我的爱
对这毛把手
对这杯毒酒

我该带上谁
去绝望边缘
顶在她心上
吻她的毛发

所以我会拿出所有爱
我会将它一分为二
一半给你
一半给我

我们会饮下毒酒
我们会藏起棒子
爱人会呻吟
另一个将会笑

我会爬上你的床
我会躺在你身旁
我会把骨头埋掉
我会娶你做新娘

当你来到我的房间
你做的也一样
你会挖开我的泥巴地
你会埋葬你的新郎

我以这爱发誓
这爱生死相许
发誓我们将分离
发誓我们将成夫妻

——秃山，1994

83

SPLIT

What can I do
with this love of mine
with this hairy knob
with this poison wine

Who shall I take
to the edge of despair
with my knee on her heart
and my lips in her hair

So I'll take all my love
and I'll split it in two
and there's one part for me
and there's one part for you

And we'll drink the wine
and we'll hide the staff
and the lover will groan

and the other will laugh

And I'll go to your bed
and I'll lie by your side
and I'll bury the bones
and I'll marry the bride

And you'll do the same
when you come to my room
You'll dig in my dirt
and you'll bury the groom

And I swear by this love
which is living and dead
that we will be separate
and we will be wed

– Mt. Baldy, 1994

if you are
young
and you
don't hap-
pen
to be
Arthur
Rimbaud
we would
prefer
not to hear
from
you

and if you do
happen to be
Arthur
Rimbaud
we
definitely
do not
want
to
hear
from you

seal of silence

如果你还年轻
而且碰巧你不是
阿尔蒂尔·兰波
那么我们宁愿不要听到你的消息

如果碰巧你正是亚瑟·兰波
我们就坚决不想听到你的消息

沉默之印

亚历桑德拉走了
仿《上帝抛弃了安东尼》，C.卡瓦菲作

夜突然变冷。
神准备启程。
亚历桑德拉趴在他肩上，
他们溜出你心的岗亭。

被纯粹的欢乐指引，
他们得到了光，他们缠成一团；
他们在美酒欢歌中坠落
光芒四射超乎你想象。

这不是幻术，你的感觉都在骗人，
一个断续的梦，在清晨消散——
说再见吧，亚历桑德拉走了。
说再见吧，亚历桑德拉没了。

就算她把你吻醒。
就算她睡上你的绸缎。
也不要说这一刻是幻影。
不要屈从于这样的伎俩。

有人为这一切准备了很久，
稳步走到窗前。把酒喝干。
美妙的音乐。亚历桑德拉笑了。
你最初的承诺又浮上心头。

你有幸得到她的夜晚，
那荣幸让你自己复原——
说再见吧，亚历桑德拉走了。
亚历桑德拉走了，和她的上帝一道。

有人为这个机会准备了很久；
把你每个破灭的计划都握在手中——
不要找一个懦夫的借口
躲藏在因果背后。

你被一个意义纠缠，
密码已经失效，十字架也不交叉——
说再见吧，亚历桑德拉走了。
说再见吧，亚历桑德拉没了。
　　——希腊海德拉岛，1999年9月

ALEXANDRA LEAVING

after "The God Abandons Anthony," by C. Cavafy

Suddenly the night has grown colder.
Some deity preparing to depart.
Alexandra hoisted on his shoulder,
they slip between the sentries of your heart.

Upheld by the simplicities of pleasure,
they gain the light, they formlessly entwine;
and radiant beyond your widest measure
they fall among the voices and the wine.

It's not a trick, your senses all deceiving,
a fitful dream the morning will exhaust –
Say goodbye to Alexandra leaving.
Then say goodbye to Alexandra lost.

Even though she sleeps upon your satin.
Even though she wakes you with a kiss.
Do not say the moment was imagined.
Do not stoop to strategies like this.

As someone long prepared for this to happen,
Go firmly to the window. Drink it in.
Exquisite music. Alexandra laughing.
Your first commitments tangible again.

You who had the honour of her evening,
And by that honour had your own restored –
Say goodbye to Alexandra leaving.
Alexandra leaving with her lord.

As someone long prepared for the occasion;
In full command of every plan you wrecked –
Do not choose a coward's explanation
that hides behind the cause and the effect.

You who were bewildered by a meaning,
whose code was broken, crucifix uncrossed –
Say goodbye to Alexandra leaving.
Then say goodbye to Alexandra lost.

– Hydra, Greece, September 1999

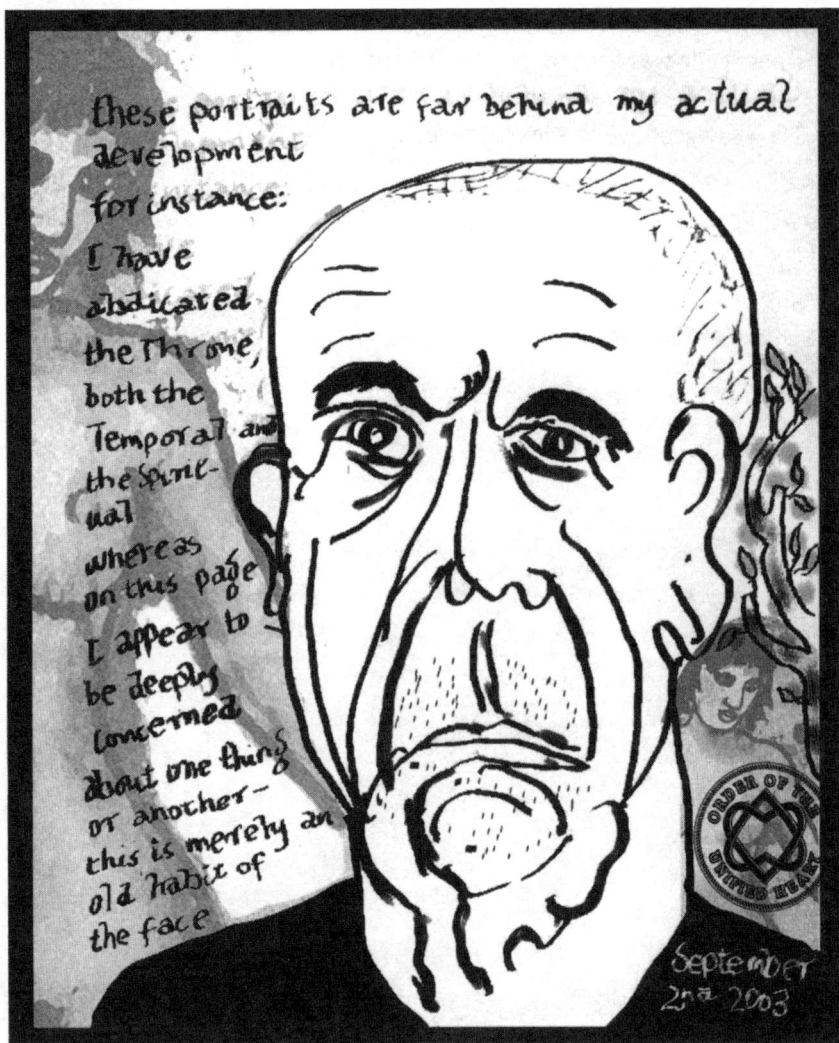

这些肖像与我的实际情况相差甚远
比如说：我已经放弃了王位，
无论是世俗的还是精神的
尽管在这一页
我看上去还是对
这样那样的事

深感兴趣
这只是一种
旧的
习惯表情

2003年9月2日

一首波多黎各人的歌

"心碎的魔鬼"
就是那首歌
一首魔鬼唱的歌
不管谁听过
都会从此变得不同
"心碎的魔鬼"
在每个听过的
男女心中
软弱的变得更软弱
基督的爱变得更强大
那夜人们在床上
紧紧相拥
仿佛其他一切都是死亡
和我一起听的
有阿曼达和奥斯卡·朵瑞特
以及凯西·翰克
以及其他许多
我再也没见过的人

A PUERTO RICAN SONG

'The Devil's Broken Heart'
that was the song
and it was the Devil singing it
and whoever heard that song
would never be the same
and in every heart
of those men and women who heard
'The Devil's Broken Heart'
the weakness weakened
and the Christ of Love strengthened
and people went to bed that night
holding on to each other
like everything else was death
I listened to it
with Armand and Oscar Dorente
and Kathy Hanking
and a lot of other people
I've never seen again

不羁街

一口酒，一根烟，
然后就该动身
我收拾好小厨房
给老班卓调好音
塞车让我误了点

不过他们给我留了座
我就是我，这样的我
回到不羁街

哦我的爱，我还记得
我们熟悉的欢乐

那些河流与瀑布
你我共浴其中
被你的美所倾倒
我甘愿跪下舔干你
的脚

通过这种种教导，你把一个男人
送上不羁街

来吧，我的朋友，别害怕
我们在这儿多么轻松
是爱造出了我们
我们消失在爱中
尽管所有血与肉的地图
都贴在门口
却没人告诉我们
不羁街有什么用

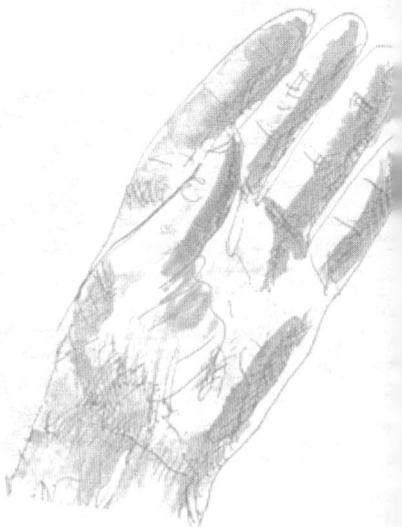

哦光的王冠，哦黑暗的神
我从未想到我们会遇见
你吻我的唇，于是尘埃落定
我回到不羁街

BOOGIE STREET

A sip of wine, a cigarette,
and then it's time to go
I tidied up the kitchenette.
I tuned the old banjo.
I'm wanted at the traffic-jam.
They're saving me a seat.
I'm what I am, and what I am,
is back on Boogie Street.

And O my love, I still recall
the pleasures that we knew;
the rivers and the waterfall
wherein I bathed with you.
Bewildered by your beauty there
I'd kneel to dry your feet.
By such instructions you prepare
a man for Boogie Street.

So come, my friends, be not afraid.
We are so lightly here.
It is in love that we are made;
in love we disappear.
Tho' all the maps of blood and flesh
are posted on the door,
there's no one who has told us yet
what Boogie Street is for.

O Crown of Light, O Darkened One,
I never thought we'd meet.
You kiss my lips, and then it's done:
I'm back on Boogie Street.

有限的程度

一旦我明白了
　（即使是在有限的程度上）
这是个上帝的世界
体重立刻
开始下降
此刻
我正穿着
六年级的
曲棍球服

A LIMITED DEGREE

As soon as I understood
(even to a limited degree)
that this is G-d's world
I began to lose weight
immediately
At this very moment
I am wearing
my hockey uniform
from the Sixth Grade

跑腿人生

如果你幸运
你会变老
并度过
你的跑腿人生。
你会察觉
人们需要什么
在他们问之前
就已经提供。
你会开着你的车
迎来送往
四处奔波
无论交通
还是天气
你都丝毫
不为所动。
你会沿着405公路
一路疾行
到圣地亚哥
因为某人的格言
去捡一颗橡果
诸如此类如此等等。
尽管你的心
在痛
为了你始终没找到的
那个女孩
为了经过
多年的
心灵苦修
你依然无法
自我顿悟
但某种愉悦
将从你破碎的
希望和向往中
开始产生。

如饥似渴
你接受了你的
下一个差事：
在拉斯维加斯的
一间失物招领处
找出
一副太阳眼镜
只要花几个小时
穿过沙漠。
你的头发白了
胸部有了赘肉
一个大肚腩
挺上裤腰带
你已经不再是男孩
或者甚至男人
但一种感激之情
使你的一举一动
都生气勃勃。
是的，先生，这就是
那副金框的墨镜
她把它忘在了吃角子老虎机
旁边的
塑料托盘。
不，先生，我没有说谎。

95

A LIFE OF ERRANDS

If You Are Lucky
You Will Grow Old
And Live
A Life Of Errands.
You Will Discern
What People Need
And Provide It
Before They Ask.
You Will Drive Your Car
Here And There
Delivering And Fetching
And Neither The Traffic
Nor The Weather
Will Bother You
In The Least.
You Will Whip Down
The 405
To San Diego
To Pick Up An Acorn
For Someone's Proverb
And So On And So Forth.
In Spite Of The Ache
In Your Heart
About The Girl You
Never Found
And The Fact That
After Years Of
Spiritual Rigour
You Did Not Manage

To Enlighten Yourself
A Certain Cheerfulness
Will Begin To
Arise Out Of Your Crushed
Hopes And Intentions.
How Thirstily
You Embrace Your
Next Commission:
To Sift Through
The Sunglasses
At A Lost And Found
In Las Vegas
Just A Few Hours
Across The Desert.
Your Hair Is White
You Have Breasts
And A Gut
Over Your Belt
You Are No Longer A Boy,
Or Even A Man
But A Sense Of Gratitude
Enlivens Every Move
You Make.
Yes, Sir, These Are The
Very Gold-Rimmed Pair
She Left In The Plastic Tray
Beside The Dollar
Slot Machines.
No, Sir, I Am Not Lying.

祝我好运

一张新鲜的蛛网
迎风招展
就像一张大三角帆
横跨打开的窗
他就在那儿
小小的船长
在一根银丝上
扬帆远航
祝我好运
海军上将
很长时间了
我什么都没干完

WISH ME LUCK

a fresh spiderweb
billowing
like a spinnaker
across the open window
and here he is
the little master
sailing by
on a thread of milk
wish me luck
admiral
I haven't finished anything
in a long time

任务

我该干活时干
该睡觉时睡
该死时死
此刻我可离去

离开需求
离开富足
精神需求
洞穴需求

爱人，我属于你
永远如此
从骨髓到毛孔
从渴望到皮肤

此刻我任务
已结束：
但愿我一生
得到宽恕

我追过的身体
也追过我
我的渴望是地点
我的死亡是帆

（北岛　译）

MISSION

I've worked at my work
I've slept at my sleep
I've died at my death
And now I can leave

Leave what is needed
And leave what is full
Need in the Spirit
And need in the Hole

Beloved, I'm yours
As I've always been
From marrow to pore
From longing to skin

Now that my mission
Has come to its end:
Pray I'm forgiven
The life that I've led

The Body I chased
It chased me as well
My longing's a place
My dying a sail

神像

过了一会儿
我开始和娃娃玩起来
我喜欢他们平静的表情
在315房间的一角
他们都有各自的位置

我会对自己说：
没关系
哪怕莱昂纳德无法呼吸
哪怕他无可救药地陷入
慌乱的处境

我会点上一支烟
和一根印度熏香
在吊扇的飞转下
两者都烧得太快

然后我也许会说
一些这样的话：
谢谢你
给我的人生条件
让事情变得一目了然
那就是我对一切
都无能为力

接下来的晚上

我会看CNN*
但现在
是用一种完全不同的
视角

one of the dolls

其中一个娃娃

---

* CNN，美国有线电视新闻网（Cable News Network）的简称。

RELIGIOUS STATUES

After a while
I started playing with dolls
I loved their peaceful expressions
They all had their places
in a corner of Room 315

I would say to myself:
It doesn't matter
that Leonard can't breathe
that he is hopelessly involved
in the panic of the situation

I'd light a cigarette
and a stick of Nag Champa
Both would burn too fast
in the draft of the ceiling fan

Then I might say
something like:
Thank You
for the terms of my life
which make it so painlessly clear
that I am powerless
to do anything

and I'd watch CNN
the rest of the night
but now
from a completely different
point of view

怎么了

一个熟人告诉我
伟大的圣人
萨伽达塔·马哈拉吉
有次递给他一支烟，
"谢谢你，先生，但我不抽烟。"
"不抽烟？"大师说，
　　"那活着干吗？"

WHAT DID IT

An acquaintance told me
that the great sage
Nisargadatta Maharaj
once offered him a cigarette,
"Thank you, sir, but I don't smoke."
"Don't smoke?" said the master,
　　"What's life for?"

香烟问题

又开始了
像第一次一样
女孩的名字叫克莱尔
是个法国人
但这一次
男孩的名字叫自闲
是个老人

但完全一样的
是香烟的
承诺，美丽
和拯救
一包打开的香烟
小小的帕台农神庙*

地点不再是希腊
而是印度
一个用来不快乐的新地方
但这一次
这个男孩没有因为他的不快乐
而不快乐
克莱尔也注意到了
这个男孩
已经六十五

而孟买，正如四十年前的
雅典
是一座适合抽烟的城市

好了，现在已经够了
凭着我书本上的经验
我能爱她
同时也爱我的余生

---

* 帕台农神庙（Parthenon），雅典卫城主体建筑，为了歌颂雅典战胜波斯侵略者的胜利而建，是供奉雅典娜女神的最大神殿，帕台农原意为贞女，是雅典娜的别名。

THE CIGARETTE ISSUE

This is beginning again
and like the first time
the girl's name is Claire
and she's French
But this time
the boy's name is Jikan
and he's an old man

It's not Greece any more
it's India
the new place for unhappiness
but this time
the boy is not unhappy
with his unhappiness
and Claire also has noticed
that the boy

is sixty-five years old

But what is exactly the same
is the promise, the beauty
and the salvation
of cigarettes
the little Parthenon
of an opened pack of cigarettes

and Mumbai, like the Athens
of forty years ago
is a city to smoke in

Well, that's enough for now
I will be able to love her
and also love the rest of my life
from my experience with books

我想念妈妈

我想带她去印度
给她买
黄金和珠宝
我想听她哀叹
街上的贫民
听她惊叹
阿拉伯海
无情的灰暗
她在所有事上都是对的
包括对我那把愚蠢的吉他
和它会把我带向何方
她会弄懂其中的意思
对那些棉布旗帜
那些港口的悲伤
那些往事的拱门
她会拍拍我的小脑袋
为我的脏歌祝福

I MISS MY MOTHER

I want to bring her to India
And buy her
Gold and jewels
I want to hear her sigh
For the poor in the street
And marvel
At the unforgiving greyness
Of the Arabian Sea
She was right about everything
Including my foolish guitar
And where it got me
She would make sense of
The cotton flags
The sorrows of the port
The arches of the past
She'd pat my little head
And bless my dirty song

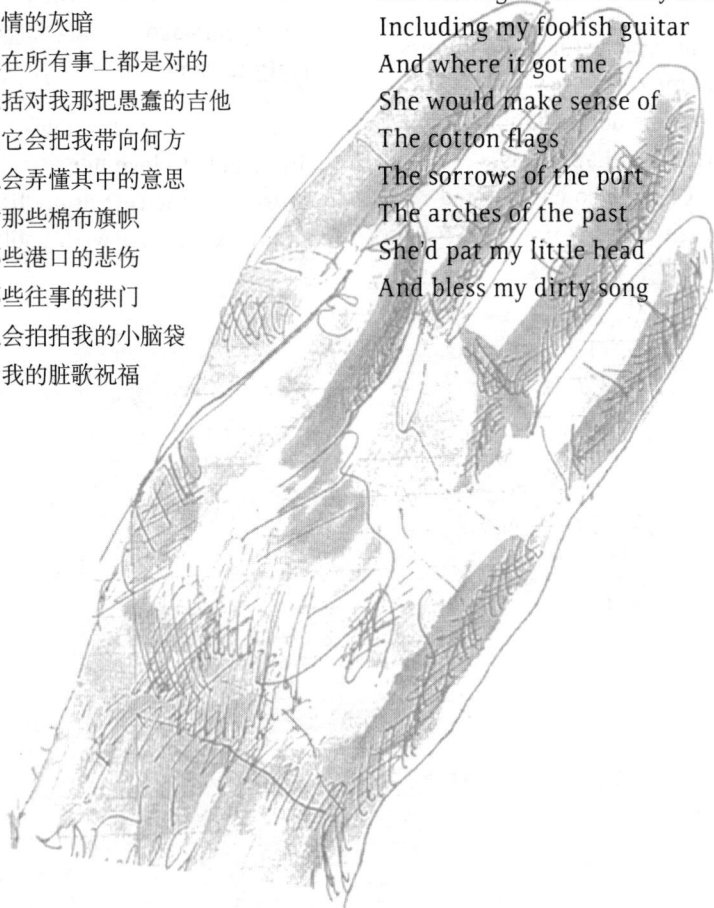

千千万万

在千千万万
被当成，
或想被当成
诗人的家伙中，
也许有一两个
是真的
其余都是假货，
围着圣地乱转
想让自己看上去像是真的。
不用说
我就是假货之一，
这就是我的故事。

THOUSANDS

Out of the thousands
who are known,
or who want to be known
as poets,
maybe one or two
are genuine
and the rest are fakes,
hanging around the sacred precincts
trying to look like the real thing.
Needless to say
I am one of the fakes,
and this is my story.

我的宝贝儿不在

我的宝贝儿不在
当我去试探她的爱
我祈求上帝保佑
今天她会出现

我只要偷偷看上两眼
如果看见她被融化
我就知道
我的感觉不假

我的心像荆棘
她的心像大树
我的心又干又刺
她的心如华盖

我一整夜没睡
却只想到这些
我知道这不对
但没什么真的正确

她正站在她的"机器"旁
我会小心翼翼地穿过走道
如果不出意料
她会向我致以微笑

于是我就会十分幸福
我就能再活一天
我将感谢她的施舍
然后挣扎着离开

MY BABY WASN'T THERE

My Baby wasn't there
When I went to test Her love
But She'll be there today
I pray to G-d above

I'll sneak a look or two
And if I see Her melt
I'll know that it was true
This feeling that I felt

My heart is like a thorn
Hers is like a Tree
My heart is dry and torn
Hers a Canopy

I've been up all night
And all I've got is this
I know that it's not right
But nothing really is

She's there at Her Machine
I'll tiptoe down the aisle
And if it's meant to be
She'll greet me with a Smile

Then I'll be so happy
I'll live another day
I'll thank Her for Her Charity
And then I'll limp away

杜斯科的小酒馆1967

他们还在下面杜斯科的店里吟唱，
在恒星和流星的深夜
坐在古老的松树下。
如果你走到窗边，你就能听见。
那是某个人婚礼的尾声，
或者也可能一个男孩要在早上搭船离开。
桌子上有你一个位置，
有你的酒，和大陆来的苹果，
歌里有空隙留给你的声音。
随便披上件什么，
不管是谁你都必须告诉他
你正要出发，
告诉他，或者带上他，但要快：
他们已经派人来找你——
已经听得见呼喊——
他们不会永远等你。
甚至现在他们已经不再等了。

DUSKO'S TAVERNA 1967

They are still singing down at Dusko's,
sitting under the ancient pine tree,
in the deep night of fixed and falling stars.
If you go to your window you can hear them.
It is the end of someone's wedding,
or perhaps a boy is leaving on a boat in the morning.
There is a place for you at the table,
wine for you, and apples from the mainland,
a space in the songs for your voice.
Throw something on,
and whoever it is you must tell
that you are leaving,
tell them, or take them, but hurry:
they have sent for you –
the call has come –
they will not wait forever.
They are not even waiting now.

不合适

这不合适
在一个娱乐场所
发现你的身影
试图忘记
过去亿万年的
小小恐怖

首先
我不喜欢勇敢的小提琴
刮擦着
大屠杀的边
仿佛在暗示
刽子手很软弱
受害者将会赢
它用一个梦
把噩梦复杂化
它把噩梦
翻了个里朝外
扔掉小提琴

也打消你的勇气
你有没有注意到
那些暴徒
和噬血者
如何被你的勇气所吸引
在他们看来
那是一种挑衅

把它还给石头
还给泥土

还给支撑泥土的东西
用人心
结束这丑陋的实验

请别再跟我提起
那座孤单的火车站
就在那儿,一阵苹果籽的冰雹中
我们互相脱掉了衣裳

而这愚昧谅解的
声音——
经受着深深的羞辱
当潮水般的沉默
拒绝承认

站在那儿别动
在你孤独的
虚荣之中
召集短命的眼泪
肤浅的笑声
及安慰

109

来拥抱你的失败
来服从你的苦痛

站在那儿别动
骄傲自大，昂首挺胸
　　让人起鸡皮疙瘩的家伙
披着宗教的

性感碎布

我衷心地希望
我们不必
在下一次游乐中重逢

　　　　　　　　　　——1979

UNBECOMING

It's unbecoming
to find you
in a place of entertainment
trying to forget
the tiny horror
of the last million years

Most of all
I dislike the brave violin
scraping against
the side of the massacre
as if to infer
that the killers are weak
and the victims will win
It complicates the nightmare
with a dream
It turns the nightmare
outside-in
Discard the violin

And put away your courage
Haven't you noticed
how the thugs
and the blood-drinkers
are drawn to your courage
It is a provocation
in their sight

Give it back to the rocks
to the mud
to that which supports the mud
End this ugly experiment

with the human heart

Please do not tell me again
about the lonely railway station
where we undressed each other
in a hail of apple seeds
And this voice of ignorant
understanding –
experience the deep humiliation
as the tidal silence
refuses to affirm it

Stand there
in the vanity
of your solitude
Summon the short-lived tears
the shallow laughter
the comforts
that obey your suffering
that embrace your defeat

Stand there
goosefleshed and proud
        high-breasted one
in the erotic rags
of religion

I sincerely hope
we do not have to meet again
at the next amusement

    – 1979

111

23街上的老自助餐馆

我逛进那家自助餐馆
头上戴着某种宗教帽
肉丸子圆溜溜
薄煎饼平展展
我请求在天堂的上帝
让这里保持原状

——1970

THE OLD AUTOMAT ON 23RD ST.

I wandered into the Automat
Wearing a kind of religious hat
The meatballs were round
And the pancakes were flat
I asked G-d in heaven
To keep it like that

– 1970

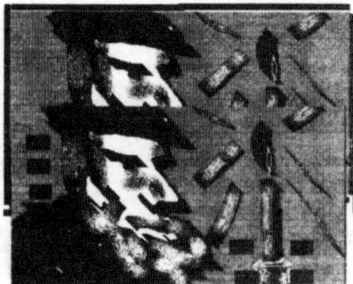

Paris again
the great Mouth Culture
oysters and cheese
explanations to everyone

又是巴黎　　　牡蛎和奶酪
伟大的嘴文化　对每个人解释

太老

我太老
老得已经不知道
那些新杀手的名字
比如这位
看上去疲倦而迷人
聚精会神，一副专家风度
他看上去很像我
像我正在
向无可救药的疯子
讲解佛教的一种激进形式
他以古老的
高等法术的名义
发号施令
多少人家被活活烧死
多少儿童变成残废
他也许还听过
一两首我写的歌
他们所有人
所有这些双手血淋淋的刽子手
这些嚼心肝的家伙
这些剥头皮的机器
他们全都在
随着披头士的音乐起舞
他们崇拜鲍勃·迪伦
亲爱的朋友
我们只剩下极少数几个
沉默着
不停地颤抖着
躲在血泊中——
让狂热分子大吃一惊

当我们彼此作证
为那古老的暴行
那古老而陈旧的暴行
它们驱散了
心温暖的渴望
心谦卑的进化
把祈祷
变成一场呕吐

TOO OLD

I am too old
to learn the names
of the new killers
This one here
looks tired and attractive
devoted, professorial
He looks a lot like me
when I was teaching
a radical form of Buddhism
to the hopelessly insane
In the name of the old
high magic
he commands
families to be burned alive
and children mutilated
He probably knows
a song or two that I wrote
All of them
all the bloody hand bathers
and the chewers of entrails
and the scalp peelers
they all danced
to the music of the Beatles
they worshipped Bob Dylan
Dear friends
there are very few of us left
silenced
trembling all the time
hidden among the blood –
stunned fanatics
as we witness to each other
the old atrocity
the old obsolete atrocity
that has driven out
the heart's warm appetite
and humbled evolution
and made a puke of prayer

卡米尼海滩

帆船
　　银浪
她睫毛上的
　　水晶盐粒
整个世界
　　突然　发亮
一瞬间　面对上帝
　　让你转向内心

THE BEACH AT KAMINI

The sailboats
　　the silver water
the crystals of salt
　　on her eyelashes
All the world
　　sudden and shining
the moment before G-d
　　turned you inward

白天

我坐在这儿
在窗边
等着你
身穿十字架的制服
慢跑着经过
你让我想起了自己
也许（我漫无目的地猜想）
我可以抚慰你
我喜欢你眉间的皱纹
和被忧虑蹂躏的痕迹
越过你紧锁的表情
你有了新的面孔
即将到来的面孔
没有感觉的面孔
你选择了力量的道路
通向你的悲伤
在每个人心里
你都是那么私密
我向你致敬
勇敢的灵魂
你忍受了那么多
却享受得那么少。

my secret drug is death
I take it whenever I see you
and you don't see me

死亡是我的秘密毒品
每当我看见你
而你却没有看见我
我就吸上一点
03/11/2

2/11/03

DURING THE DAY

I sit here
At the window
Waiting for you
To come jogging past
In your crucifix uniform
You remind me of myself
Perhaps (I wonder aimlessly)
I could comfort you
I love the furrows between your eyes
And the ravages of anxiety
Across your clenched expression
You have the new face
The coming face
The face of no objective experience
And you have chosen the path of muscle
Toward your sorrow
How private you are
In the minds of everyone
I salute you
Brave spirit
Who has swallowed so much
And tasted so little.

先贤祠*里的笑声

LAUGHTER IN THE PANTHEON

我喜欢那笑声
　　老诗人们
当你们欢迎我到来

但我不会在这儿
　　停留太久
你们也不会
　　　　——1985

I enjoyed the laughter
　　　　old poets
as you welcomed me

but I won't be staying
　　　　here for long
You won't be either

　　　　– 1985

---

* 先贤祠位于巴黎市中心塞纳河左岸的拉丁区，是永久纪念法国历史名人的圣殿。它原是路易十五时代建成的圣热内维耶瓦教堂，1791年被收归国有脱离宗教后，改为埋葬伟人的墓地。先贤祠内安葬着伏尔泰，卢梭，雨果，柏辽兹，大仲马等著名艺术家。

亲爱的日记

你比《圣经》
《飞鸟大会》*
和《奥义书》**
全部加起来
还要伟大

你比《圣经》经文
和汉谟拉比法典
还要严厉
比钉在大教堂门上的
路德传单还要危险

你比《雅歌》***
更甜蜜
比《吉尔伽美什史诗》****
更有力
比冰岛的萨迦*****
更勇敢

对那些为了
严守秘密
每天的秘密
而献出生命的人
我垂首感恩

亲爱的日记
我没有不敬的意思
但你比任何圣典
都更崇高

有时哪怕一份
我的活动清单
也比《人权法案》******更神圣
更令人震撼

(孔亚雷　译)

---

* 《飞鸟大会》，12世纪的一部波斯诗集，总长约4 500行。
** 《奥义书》，印度最经典的古老哲学著作。
*** 《雅歌》，《圣经·旧约》诗歌智慧书的第五卷，主要描写男女间爱情的欢悦与忧愁。
**** 《吉尔伽美什史诗》，来自四大古文明之一的美索不达米亚的文学作品。史诗所述的历史时期据信在公元前2700年至公元前2500年之间，比已知最早的写成文字的文学作品早200到400年。
***** 萨迦，13世纪前后冰岛和挪威人用文字记载的古代民间口传故事，主要包括神话和历史传奇。
****** 《人权法案》，指美国宪法中第一至第十条宪法修正案，包括言论、新闻、宗教与集社等方面的自由与权利。

DEAR DIARY

You are greater than the Bible
And the Conference of the Birds
And the Upanishads
All put together

You are more severe
Than the Scriptures
And Hammurabi's Code
More dangerous than Luther's paper
Nailed to the Cathedral door

You are sweeter
Than the Song of Songs
Mightier by far
Than the Epic of Gilgamesh
And braver
Than the Sagas of Iceland

I bow my head in gratitude
To the ones who give their lives
To keep the secret
The daily secret
Under lock and key

Dear Diary
I mean no disrespect
But you are more sublime
Than any Sacred Text

Sometimes just a list
Of my events
Is holier than the Bill of Rights
And more intense

寒冷

寒冷抓住我
我发抖
酒
胜过我的泪
夜把我放上床
悲伤
坚定我的决心
你名字燃烧
在雕像下
每当和你一起
我要在那儿
雨为我宽衣解带
风为你的缺席
赋予形状
我进出
那一颗心
不再为自由
挣扎

（北岛　译）

THE COLD

The cold seizes me
and I shiver
The wine
overthrows my tears
The night puts me to bed
and the sorrows
strengthen my resolve
Your name is burning
under a statue
Even when I was with you
I wanted to be here
The rain unhooks my belt
The wind gives a shape
to your absence
I move in and out
of the One Heart
no longer struggling
to be free

魔药

我起得太晚
一天已经没了
我不怪公鸡
也没泼水洗脸
接着天就黑了
我逛遍了圣德尼街*的
每个角落
我甚至跟其他败家子

聊起了宗教
他们，像我一样，在忙着泡妞
为了寻找一种魔药
我在床上看一首赞美诗
看到一半
就睡着了

——蒙特利尔，1975

A MAGIC CURE

I get up too late
The day is lost
I don't bless the rooster
I don't raise my hands to the water
Then it's dark
and I look into all the spots
on rue St-Denis
I even talk religion
to the other wastrels
who, like me, are after new women
In bed I fall asleep
in the middle of a Psalm
which I am reading
for a magic cure

– Montreal, 1975

---

* 圣德尼街（rue St-Denis），加拿大蒙特利尔市著名的酒吧一条街。

the truth of
the line

overwhelms
all other

considerations

1/24/03

线条*的真理压倒了所有其他考虑
03/1/24

---

*原文为the line，有多种含义，既可指作画的线条，也可指歌词、诗行，或者摆放成
一条细线准备吸食的可卡因。

莱顿的问题

每次我告诉他
接下来我想干什么，
莱顿就严肃地问：
莱昂纳德，你确定
你做的是错的吗？

IRVING

– *after a photo by Laszlo*

欧文
——据拉兹罗所拍照片

LAYTON'S QUESTION

Always after I tell him
what I intend to do next,
Layton solemnly inquires:
Leonard, are you sure
you're doing the wrong thing?

如果你知道

如果你知道我们有多爱你
你就会掩饰
你就不会到处乱来
不会满怀激情地
在广岛
杀死三十万人
或从月亮上铲起岩石
碾得粉碎
寻找你
寻找你那失落的鼓舞

IF YOU KNEW

if you knew how much we loved you
you'd cover up
you wouldn't fuck around
with the passion
that killed three hundred thousand people
at hiroshima
or scooped up rocks from the moon
and crushed them into dust
looking for you
looking for your lost encouragement

我为爱而写

我为爱而写。
接着我为钱而写。
对于像我这样的人
这是一回事。

——1975

I WROTE FOR LOVE

I wrote for love.
Then I wrote for money.
With someone like me
it's the same thing.

– 1975

因为梦见你，他们给了我一枚奖章

洛尔迦*还活着

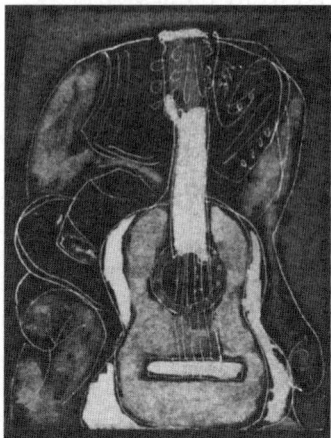

LORCA LIVES

Lorca lives in New York City
He never went back to Spain
He went to Cuba for a while
But he's back in town again

He's tired of the gypsies
And he's tired of the sea
He hates to play his old guitar
It only has one key

He heard that he was shot and killed
He never was, you know
He lives in New York City
He doesn't like it though

洛尔迦住在纽约
他再也没回过西班牙
他去了一阵子古巴
但很快又回来了

他已经厌倦了吉卜赛
他也厌倦了海
他讨厌再弹他的旧吉他
那玩意只有一个调儿

他听说他被枪杀了
根本没那回事，你知道
他还住在纽约
尽管他也不喜欢这儿

---

* 洛尔迦，全名为费德里科·加西亚·洛尔迦 (Federico Garcia Lorca, 1898—1936) 被称为20世纪最伟大的西班牙诗人。他的诗结合了西班牙民间歌谣的特点，节奏优美哀婉，想象力极其丰富，具有强烈生动的色彩感和形象感，在世界诗坛有极大影响。

仁慈把我还给了

一个我想要的女人——
一项我垂涎的荣誉——
一处我想让心停驻的地方——
然后仁慈把我还给了
三和弦
与歌的转折

MERCY RETURNS ME

A woman I want –
An honour I covet –
A place where I want my mind to dwell –
Then Mercy returns me
To the triad
And the crisis of the song.

传统

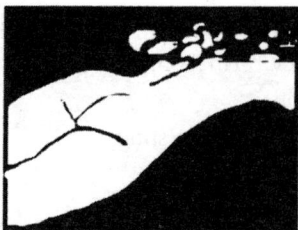

收音机里的爵士乐
书桌抽屉里的32型手枪
手里的画笔
伤感迷乱的心
他画了一个女人
萨克斯风说画得比以前好
三月寒冷的夜说画得比以前好
除了他的心和手所有东西
都说他画得比以前好
现在纸上有了一个女人
现在有了色彩
现在有了她腰部的阴影
他了解自己的同伴
那些惊喜
来自耐心和混乱的寂寞
他知道频率

通过他的电台
怎样去让那些
他不会弹的变化
把他连接到会弹的人那儿
而这个纸上的女人
她的美丽永不会刺破空气
她也属于这里
在巨大博物馆的地下室
她也有她的位置
并不是说他就能以此炫耀
哪怕是对他自己
也不是说他敢称其为
某种途径
他永远不会解脱
或改善
他的处境
那把他和这孤独紧紧绑在一起
或者，带着爱意俯身
领悟这突然而来的仁慈
这仁慈涌入房间
并立刻将它融入
传统的金色光线中

THE TRADITION

Jazz on the radio
32 in the desk drawer
Brush in hand
Heart in sad confusion
He draws a woman
The sax says it better
The cold March night says it better
Everything but his heart and his hand
Says it better
Now there is a woman on the paper
Now there are colours
Now there is a shadow on her waist
He knows his own company
The surprises
Of patience and disorderly solitude
Knows the tune
According to his station
How to let the changes
He can't play
Connect him to the ones who can
And the woman on the paper
Who will never pierce the air with her beauty
She belongs here too
She too has her place
In the basement of the vast museum
Not that he could boast about it
Even to himself
Not that he would dare to call it
Some kind of Path
He will never untangle
Or upgrade
The circumstances
That fasten him to this loneliness

Or bent down with love
Comprehend the sudden mercy
Which floods the room
And dissolves it now
In the traditional golden light

My Metal Cup

我的金属杯

德国好人

你带我去见你家人
特意先再三提醒
你父亲是个法西斯
你母亲是个鸡

我有点儿失望
我都懒得说实话：
你父母他们只是些德国好人
但你，你是个希特勒青年军

所以我打算住到中国
住在那儿更划算
那儿的刽子手是个诗人
而你的同志是个姑娘

——1973

GOOD GERMANS

You took me to your family
You warned me well before
that your father is a fascist
and your mother is a whore

I was kind of disappointed
I was bored to tell the truth:
your folks they're just Good Germans
but you, you're Hitler Youth

So I'm going to live in China
where you get a better deal
where your killer is a poet
and your comrade is a girl

– 1973

如果我能帮你

如果我能帮你，老兄，我会帮的
我真的会
我会为你祈祷
我会让你虎背熊腰
只要有一点可能
你会喜欢
我就带你去一座桥
人们都说它很美
我会送你那辆摩托车
如果你是名歌手
我会在自动点唱机里点你的歌
我会帮你跨越
人生中的那道坎
我愿意为你再次被钉死在十字架
我愿意为你做所有这一切
因为我是你的上帝
但你已经走得离我那么远
我只好用我最隐晦的方式
在此将你拥抱
你一直希望自己勇敢而真实
那么现在做个深呼吸
用猛烈的孤独
开始你伟大的历险

IF I COULD HELP YOU

If I could help you, buddy, I would
I really would
I'd pray for you
I'd make muscles appear on your back
I'd take you to a bridge
that people think is beautiful
if there were the slightest chance
that you'd like it
I'd get you that motorcycle
I'd put your songs on the jukebox
if you were a singer
I'd help you step across
that crack in your life
I'd die for you on the cross again
I would do all these things for you
because I'm the Lord of your life
but you've gone so far from me
that I've decided to embrace you here
with my most elusive qualities
You always wanted to be brave and true
So breathe deeply now
and begin your great adventure
with crushing solitude

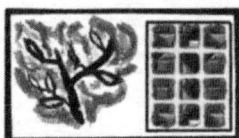

a private gaze

even though he was built to see the world this way, he was also built to disregard, to be free of the way he was built to see the world

一次个人凝视
哪怕他天生就这样看世界，但他也天生就藐视陈规，不按天生看世界的方式去看世界

遥控器

我经常想起你
当我一个人躺在
房间里张着
嘴而遥控器
掉在床上的什么地方

（孔亚雷　译）

THE REMOTE

I often think about you
when I'm lying alone in
my room with my mouth
open and the remote
lost somewhere in the bed

色情迷雾

当你沉浮在色情
迷雾中
和你关于婚姻
及杂交的话一起
我只不过是
五十七岁男孩
试图在慢车道
挣点快钱

虽说晚十年
但我最终得到
左翼教派中
最漂亮的女孩
和她嘴唇去
没太阳的角落

歌唱的艺术
与生俱来
咖啡为我而死
我从不接听
任何电话
我为打电话
未留言者
祈祷

这是我洛杉矶
的生活
当你慢慢
退去黄毛衣
对你男孩般的屁股
垂涎欲滴

我试着做
丈夫
为你阴暗母性的
意向

感谢你
让我完成
那些沉闷的歌
代替更多
干你
你准许我
在黑禅垫上
激发我失败的
贵族家谱
去战胜粗俗
用铁丝网
和韵律
节拍
让美国诚实

如今我们离去

137

我有一千年
告诉你我如何
与万物上升
我如何成为
你所要的情人
除了你的美
我没别的生活
我弯曲赤裸
在你欲望配额下
我有一千年
成你的双胞胎
爱着镜中的
另一个你

最终很顺手
用我的拍立得
哄你摆姿势
当你用脏话
激怒
我的助听器

你的狂热不再催我
我的狂热和垂落的
肩膀
我们无耻的生命
是谷物
为奉献洒落
在爱情蹒跚的
高地前
你焦虑另一面
是汗的吊床
呻吟
世代蝴蝶
交媾死亡

我们消除差异
时光流逝
如上帝最小宠物
舔我们手指
当我们沉睡
在皮带手镯的
纠葛中
最初之夜多甜蜜
二十三夜
死与苦以后的
夜
今早的甜蜜
蜂群涌进
蜀葵
桌上物件的
完美秩序
无足轻重的
所有古老意愿
当我们消除
当我们消除
每个差异

（北岛　译）

THE MIST OF PORNOGRAPHY

when you rose out of the mist
of pornography
with your talk of marriage
and orgies
I was a mere boy
of fifty-seven
trying to make a fast buck
in the slow lane

it was ten years too late
but I finally got
the most beautiful girl
on the religious left
to go with her lips
to the sunless place

the art of song
was in my bones
the coffee died for me
I never answered
any phone calls
and I said a prayer
for whoever called
and didn't leave a message

this was my life
in Los Angeles
when you slowly
removed your yellow sweater
and I slobbered over
your boyish haunches
and I tried to be
a husband
to your dark and motherly
intentions

I thank you
for the ponderous songs
I brought to completion
instead of ----ing you
more often
and the hours you allowed me
on a black meditation mat
intriguing with my failed
aristocratic pedigree
to overthrow vulgarity
and set America straight
with the barbed wire
and the regular beatings
of rhyme

and now that we are gone
I have a thousand years
to tell you how I rise
on everything that rises
how I became that lover
whom you wanted
who has no other life
but your beauty
who is naked and bent

under the quotas of your desire
I have a thousand years
to be your twin
the loving mirrored one
who was born with you

I'm free at last
to trick you into posing
for my Polaroid
while you inflame

my hearing aid
with your vigorous obscenities

your panic cannot hurry me here
and my panic and my falling
shoulders
our shameless lives
are the grains
scattered for an offering
before the staggering heights
of our love
and the other side of your anxiety
is a hammock of sweat
and moaning
and generations of the butterfly
mate and fall
as we undo the differences
and time comes down
like the smallest pet of G-d

to lick our fingers
as we sleep
in the tangle
of straps and bracelets
and Oh the sweetness of first nights
and twenty-third nights
and nights
after death and bitterness
sweetness of this very morning
the bees slamming into
the broken hollyhocks
and the impeccable order
of the objects on the table
the weightless irrelevance
of all our old intentions
as we undo
as we undo
every difference

the
promise
of a
youthful
shirt

Montreal
2003
Winter

一件青春衬衫的承诺
　　蒙特利尔　2003　冬

拖

"我可以坚持很久；直到水
淹没他们的河岸
冲破他们的堤坝，我才会说。"

这样，我就可以把这本书一直拖到
二十世纪末之后很久。

DELAY

"I can hold in a great deal; I don't speak
until the waters overflow their banks
and break through the dam."

Thus I was able to delay this book well beyond
the end of the 20th century.

蒙特利尔的午后

亨利和我
头上戴着帽子
在写诗
祈祷书打开着
收音机在响
亨利说：他们
弹得不对，
应该更快一点。
厨房门开着
外面在下雨
亨利说：我很抱歉杀死了你父亲
那是个打猎的意外
泽尔金拉比*正在快速
穿过湿淋淋的城市
向我们走来
带着他在电话里
答应我们的
羊毛祈祷披巾
亨利说：在
一百六十万
零两百二十九年
你会开始写一篇
《摩西五经》**的注解
而在一万四千
四百四十三年
我会开始写一篇
《摩西五经》的注解
我会称自己那篇为"青柔·青
美·哈·耶拉克"
意思是

HENRY'S ARM

亨利的胳膊

144

绿叶约定的绿
然后我们会一起写本书
名字叫《橡果和其他树叶》
　　　　或者
《阳光下的青山》
我们抽着普雷尔牌香烟
喝着热水
等待着泽尔金拉比
亨利说：我很抱歉杀死了你父亲
那是个打猎的意外
但他会回来的
伊丽莎白女王一世也会

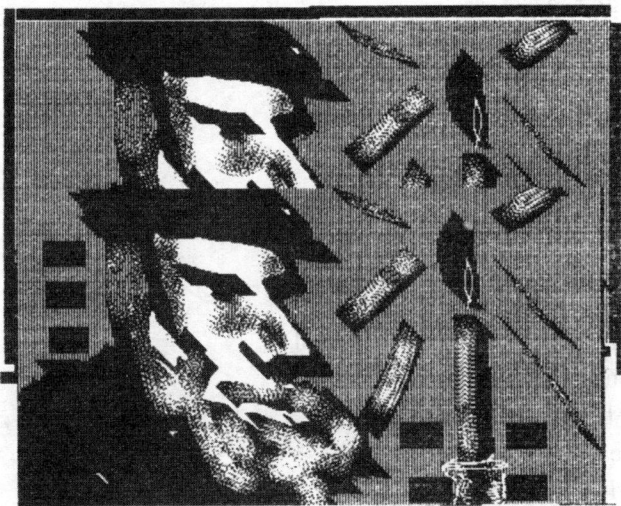

---

* 拉比（Rabbi），犹太教律法专家，希伯来文中意为师傅或教师，他们除了教导犹太人学习律法、遵行律法之外，还对律法进行诠释、评注。
** 《摩西五经》（Chumash），《圣经·旧约》最初的五部经典，用犹太人最古老的希伯来文写成，是犹太教经典中最重要的部分。

MONTREAL AFTERNOON

Henry and I
cover our heads
and write a few poems
The prayer book is open
The radio is playing
Henry says: They're not
playing that right,
it should be faster.
The kitchen door is open
It's raining
Henry says: I'm sorry I killed your father
It was a hunting accident
Rabbi Zerkin is speeding
toward us
through the wet city
with the woollen prayer-shawls
that he promised us
on the telephone
Henry says: In the year
sixteen hundred thousand
two hundred and twenty-nine
you will begin a commentary
on the Chumash
and in the year fourteen thousand
four hundred and forty-three
I will begin a commentary
on the Chumash
I'll call mine Tzim Tzimay Ha Yerak
which means
The Contracted Greens of the Greenery;

then we will write a book together
called Acorns and Other Leaves
                or
The Green Hills of Sunshine
We smoke Players Medium
drink cups of hot water
waiting for Rabbi Zerkin
Henry says: I'm sorry I killed your father
It was a hunting accident
But he'll be back
So will Queen Elizabeth the First

为首相念诗

他亲切而威严。
他让我为他念
一首诗。接着他让我
再念一首。然后又一首。
那是在南希家的屋顶上,
她管它叫"消防站"。
南希请我们吃了午饭,于是
我又念了更多的诗。随后
许多哀伤降临到他们俩
身上。

大众
情人
之死

(孔亚雷　译)

需要速度

需要速度
需要酒
需要快感
在我脊椎中

需要你的手
帮我取出
需要你的汁液
在我的猪嘴

需要看到
我熟视无睹
你需要我的
生猛欲望

需要由你
召唤我
像月亮在
聚合之海上

需要听到
我孤陋寡闻
在我耳边
你的脏字

需要知道
我一无所知
潮汐牵拽
来自你

需要感觉
未有的感觉
你的磁力
吸引我

它如今退色
它如今流逝
荷尔蒙的狂暴
不平静的歌

（北岛　译）

NEED THE SPEED

need the speed
need the wine
need the pleasure
in my spine

need your hand
to pull me out
need your juices
on my snout

need to see
I never saw
your need for me
your longing raw

need to hear
I never heard
against my ear
your dirty word

need to have
you summon me
like moon above
the gathered sea

need to know
I never knew
the tidal tow-
ing come from you

need to feel
I never felt
your magnet pull-
ing at my self

now it fades
now it's gone
hormonal rage
unquiet song

我怎能怀疑

我不再找你
我不再等你
我不再为你而死
我开始为自己而死
我飞快地变老
变得满脸肥肉
肚皮松弛
我已经忘了我曾爱过你
我老了
没有焦点，没有任务
四处游荡吃喝然后去买
越来越大的衣服
我已经忘了为什么痛恨
每一段要我自己填满的漫长空闲
今晚你为什么要回到我身边
我甚至没法从这把椅子里站起
泪水滚下我的脸颊
我重新陷入爱里
我可以就这样活下去

HOW COULD I HAVE DOUBTED

I stopped looking for you
I stopped waiting for you
I stopped dying for you
and I started dying for myself
I aged rapidly
I became fat in the face
and soft in the gut
and I forgot that I'd ever loved you
I was old
I had no focus, no mission
I wandered around eating and buying
bigger and bigger clothes
and I forgot why I hated
every long moment that was mine to fill
Why did you come back to me tonight
I can't even get off this chair
Tears run down my cheeks
I am in love again
I can live like this

欧洲上空一架飞机里的口述

莱昂纳德，
我不再孤单。
现在我将接受你的友谊
如果你能说出
一些真正关于我的事。
没错，
我有一件红色开衫
以前经常在
晚上穿。
岁月让我们走到了一起。
将你的椅背竖直。
你正在降落到维也纳
一九六二年
我在那儿杀死了自己。

VOICE DICTATING IN A PLANE OVER EUROPE

Leonardos,
I am no longer lonely.
I will accept your friendship now
if you can say
something true about me.
That is correct,
I had a red cardigan sweater
which I used to wear
in the evenings.
The years have brought us together.
Straighten your seat back.
You are landing in Vienna
where I killed myself
in nineteen sixty-two.

大事件

它即将发生。将终止所有恐怖的大事件。将终止所有悲伤的大事件。下个礼拜二，当太阳落山，我将倒弹《月光奏鸣曲》。这将逆转过去两百亿年来世界疯狂陷入苦难所带来的影响。那将是个多么迷人的夜晚。多么解脱的一声叹息，当衰老的知更鸟再次变得鲜红，当退休的夜莺重振积灰的尾翼，宣告生命万岁！

THE GREAT EVENT

It's going to happen very soon. The great event that will end the horror. That will end the sorrow. Next Tuesday, when the sun goes down, I will play the Moonlight Sonata backwards. This will reverse the effects of the world's mad plunge into suffering for the last 200 million years. What a lovely night that will be. What a sigh of relief, as the senile robins become bright red again, and the retired nightingales pick up their dusty tails, and assert the majesty of creation!

巴黎的天空

巴黎的天空
又蓝又亮
我想飞翔
用我所有的力量

她的腿很长
她的心很高
锁链强壮
但我也一样

THE PARIS SKY

The Paris sky
is blue and bright
I want to fly
with all my might

Her legs are long
her heart is high
The chains are strong
but so am I

迄今为止

我出生那天东西被吹得到处都是。那天刮大风。枯叶撞击着顺势疗法医院*的墙。我活了下来。我在惊恐中活了下来。

赐予者像支美式足球队一样在我上方挤成一团。他们开始送我东西，然后又把东西拿走。不合适的就扔回宇宙的漏斗。礼物很多，随之而来的警告也很多。

我们现在给你一颗伟大的心，但如果你喝酒，你就会开始恨这个世界。月亮是你的姐姐，但如果你吃安眠药，你就会发现自己和不幸的女人在一起。每次你想抓住爱，你就会失去一片记忆的雪花。

妈妈躺得离我不远，我听见她在哭喊，"他不是我生的！"我高贵的母亲在她的血水床上对着我一个人的耳朵哭喊。听见她的话，我用欢乐的尖叫感谢她说出真相。我不是生在一个家庭。我受到完全的保护。

铁锤到处落在婴儿的身上，但我却在一条河流上获救，在秋日美丽的埃及大地。

---

*顺势疗法18世纪由德国医生塞缪尔·哈尼曼（Samuel Hahnemann）创立，是一种不同于传统西医的医疗体系，它应用各种不同的植物、矿物或动物所制成的天然药物，以非常小的剂量来刺激与诱导病人与生俱来的免疫系统，以便自然舒缓而又迅速地治愈疾病，特别对一些疑难杂症具有明显疗效。20世纪60年代以来，在"回归自然"的潮流影响下，在西方得到广泛推广。

The Story Thus Far

Things blew all over the place on the day that I was born. It was windy. Dried leaves crashed against the walls of the Homeopathic Hospital. I was alive. I was alive in the horror.

The Givers huddled over me like a football team. They started to give me things and then to take them away. The things that didn't fit they chucked back into the Funnel of the Void. The gifts were many and many were the warnings that went with them.

We are giving you a great heart but if you drink wine you will begin to hate the world. The moon is your sister but if you take sleeping pills you will find yourself in the company of unhappy women. Every time you grab at love you will lose a snowflake of your memory.

My mother was lying not far away and I heard her cry, "He isn't mine!" My noble parent cried to my ears alone from her bed of blood and water. I heard her say it and I thanked her for the truth with a shriek of joy. I was not born into a family. I was fully protected.

The hammers fell on infants everywhere but I was saved on a river in the beautiful autumn land of Egypt.

最甜蜜的短歌

你走你的路
我也走你的路

THE SWEETEST LITTLE SONG

You go your way
I'll go your way too

东西

我就是这么一个要唱歌的东西
我爱唱
唱给我爱的其他东西
唱给我自己亲爱甜蜜的上帝
我喜欢唱给"他"和她听
唱给我宝贝私处的软毛
它如此神圣
以至于我想双膝跪地
爬着跳下一座高崖
遨游四海
在风中歌唱
风对我轻薄的灵魂
如此友好
我就是这么一个
想唱歌的东西
当我面对世人的
唾液和鄙视
哦，上帝我想唱
"我就是
这么一个要唱歌的东西"

THING

I am this thing that needs to sing
I love to sing
to my beloved's other thing
and to my own dear sweet G-d
I love to sing to Him and her
and to my baby's lower fur
which is so holy
that I want to crawl on my knees
off a high cliff
and sail around singing
in the wind
which is so friendly
to my feathery spirit
I am this thing
that wants to sing
when I am up against the spit
and scorn of judges
O G-D I want to sing
I Am
THIS THING THAT NEEDS TO SING

November 12, 1991
Los Angeles, CALIFORNIA

献给H.M.的诗

哦，完美的绅士，皇位的
拥护者；哦，西奈山*之心的
顽石；哦，凡尔登**的英雄；
我们最伟大的诗人至今还默默无闻，
他的死亡之旗一直在
贫困和孤独的荒野里飘动；
感谢你多年孤身一人
搜寻着让爱无法躲避的词句，
别无所依，除了一份赞美之情

（有一阵子我们失去了你。医生们在一个
被选中的灵魂身上尝试充满希望的科学，
但这个被选中的灵魂坐在上帝
身旁，被"他"碰了一下，便完好如初，
虽然在人们眼里，在"他"的控制下，那是破碎。）
哦，朋友，你宽恕所有来
照亮你黑暗，减弱你光环的人，
请接受对你名望这笨拙的致敬
（也别用谦虚立即提出反诉。）

我们不知是什么意志或声音
让你从高高的德科瑞高架上飞起；
我们不知是什么希伯来文让你遵从
让你把双脚抬得离沙和草那么远
想要走向空中，哦，忠实的攀鲈——

HENRY'S ARM
亨利的胳膊

161

但请祝福在那儿拯救你的主，
祝福"他的名"，"他的每个别称"，
他给了你，在那虚幻的阶梯上，
我们拥有的最勇敢的歌，关于失落，关于爱的修补。

亲爱的亨利，我知道你会原谅我写的
这一行行句子，它们笨重而古旧的调子，
因为它们是真的，而非仅仅是葬礼，
因为它们的全部辞藻都在渲染
一个对你所是男人的简单手势，
他的友谊如此珍贵，他的艺术如此纯粹，
简洁得令人晕眩，把人打翻——
我惊慌，羞愧，不得不把我的爱
藏在文学堕落的浮夸背后。

我再也不知道我要去哪儿。
我给自己找了一对桌椅。
我等待，但我不知我在等什么。
我换房间，换国家。我把我那
噼里啪啦的闪电装甲跟你比，
跟你简洁的光之武器，跟你优雅的举止——
我知道你站在我们谁也不敢站的地方，
我知道你跪在我们谁也猜不到的地方，
头脑清醒，孤身一人，巨大的心，毫不自怜。

心心相印勋章

---

* 西奈山（Sinai），《圣经》中记载的上帝授摩西十诫之处，位于埃及西奈半岛南
端，自古就被犹太教、基督教和伊斯兰教视为圣地。
** 凡尔登（Verdun），加拿大魁北克省南部的一座城市。

STANZAS FOR H.M.

O perfect gentleman, and champion
of the Royal Throne; O unbroken stone
of Sinai's heart; O Hero of Verdun;
our greatest poet until now unknown,
whose banner over death has always flown
in wilds of poverty and solitude;
I thank you for the years you spent alone
with nothing to hang on to but a mood
of glory, searching words that Love could not elude

(We lost you for a while. The doctors tried
their hopeful science on a chosen soul,
but this chosen soul was sitting by the side
of G-d, and touched by Him, hale and whole,
though broken in men's eyes, in His control.)
O friend who pardoned everyone who came
to light your dark and dim your aureole,
accept this awkward homage to your fame
(nor Modesty supply your instant counterclaim.)

We do not know the Will or voice that made
you fly from high Decarie's overpass;
we do not know the Hebrew you obeyed
to raise your feet so far from sand and grass
and try the air, O faithful Anabas –
but blessed be the One who saved you there,
and bless His Name, His every Alias,
Who gave you, on that insubstantial stair,
the bravest songs we have of loss and love's repair.
Dear Henry, I know you will forgive these
lines of mine, their clumsy antique tone,
for they are true and not mere obsequies,
and for all their rhetoric overblown
a simple gesture to the man you own,

whose friendship is so rare, whose art so pure,
simplicity is dazed, then overthrown –
alarmed and shy my love must I obscure
behind the fallen grandiose of literature.

I don't know where I'm going any more.
I find myself a table and a chair.
I wait, I don't know what I'm waiting for.
I change the room, the country. I compare
my clattering armoured blitz to your spare
weaponry of light, your refined address –
I know you stand where none of us would dare,
I know you kneel where none of us would guess,
well ordered and alone, huge heart, self-pitiless.

我为什么热爱法兰西

哦，法兰西，你把你的语言给了我孩子，把你的爱人和你的蘑菇给了我老婆。你唱我的歌。你把我的舅舅和舅妈交给纳粹。我在巴士底广场遇见警察的皮胸甲。我从共产主义者手里拿钱。我把我的中年给了吕贝隆*那些乳白色的小镇。我在鲁西戎村外的马路上逃离了几只农场犬。我的手在法兰西的大地上颤抖。我怀着一种被污染的神圣哲学走向你，你却叫我坐下来接受采访。哦，法兰西，在你那儿我被如此看重，以至于我不得不重新考虑我的位置。哦，法兰西，每个小小的弥赛亚**都要感谢你给他的孤独。我想去别的什么地方，但我总是在法兰西。要强大，要核能化，我的法兰西。要遍地风流，要谈论，谈论，永远不停地谈论怎样没有上帝地去生活。

---

* 吕贝隆（Luberon），位于法国普罗旺斯的观光胜地，有很多美丽的中世纪小镇。下文提到的鲁西戎村也是其中之一。
** 弥赛亚（Messiah）是希伯来文，与希腊文"基督"（Christ）是同义字，意为"受膏者"，古代犹太人封立君王时要在受封者头上浇香膏，所以君王也被称为"受膏者"。传说上帝将派一位受膏者来复兴犹太国，所以犹太教将 "救世主"称为"弥赛亚"。基督教认为，耶稣就是他们的弥赛亚。

WHY I LOVE FRANCE

O France, you gave your language to my children, your lovers and your mushrooms to my wife. You sang my songs. You delivered my uncle and my auntie to the Nazis. I met the leather chests of the police in Place de la Bastille. I took money from the Communists. I gave my middle age to the milky towns of the Luberon. I ran from farm dogs on a road outside of Rousillon. My hand trembles in the land of France. I came to you with a soiled philosophy of holiness, and you bade me sit down for an interview. O France, where I was taken so seriously, I had to reconsider my position. O France, every little Messiah thanks you for his loneliness. I want to be somewhere else, but I am always in France. Be strong, be nuclear, my France. Flirt with every side, and talk, talk, never stop talking about how to live without G-d.

one of those days:
when the hat doesn't help

糟糕的一天
帽子也帮不上忙

the inner sweetness
of the man
could not be
concealed

Hotel Kemps Corner
Rm 215
1/9/03

这个男人
内心的甜蜜
无法隐藏

肯普斯角旅馆　215房　03/9/1

falling in love with you

爱上你

This book will begin
to speak
when the hummingbird
comes back
to the red flower
to murder the red flower
Speak! agent
~~pages~~ of Death
Speak to the one
who loves you
the one who has failed
at love
the one you seek out
with your blurred needle

这本书将开始　　　　红花上　　　　　　对在爱上
说话　　　　　　　　要谋杀红花　　　　失败的人说
当蜂鸟　　　　　　　说吧！死亡之书之函　对你用模糊的指针
回到　　　　　　　　对爱你的人说　　　　挑出的人说

小路上

给C.C.

寂寞小路上
我来到歌之乡
并在那儿
逗留了半辈子
现在我丢下我的吉他
和电子琴
朋友和性伙伴
我再次蹒跚着
走到寂寞小路上
我老了但我不后悔
一点也不
哪怕我愤怒而孤单
充满恐惧和欲望
弯腰吻我吧
从你的迷雾从你的藤蔓
哦，崇高的主，修长的手指
深邃的凝视
弯腰吻这装着毒药和烂牙的
臭皮囊
把你的唇印上
我的心之光

ON THE PATH

for C.C.

On the path of loneliness
I came to the place of song
and tarried there
for half my life
Now I leave my guitar
and my keyboards
my friends and s-x companions
and I stumble out again
on the path of loneliness
I am old but I have no regrets
not one
even though I am angry and alone
and filled with fear and desire
Bend down to me
from your mist and vines
O high one, long-fingered
and deep-seeing
Bend down to this sack of poison
and rotting teeth
and press your lips
to the light of my heart

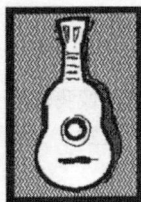

我的救世主

我时刻想着你
但我再也不能提起
我必须秘密地去爱你
我必须一个人的时候才去
就像现在
即使现在我也必须小心
我想要所有
你按你的样子造出的女人
那就是为什么
在街头经过她们身边
我要低下眼睛
你能听见我的祈祷
我无法形容的主
我无法说出的名
我为情所困
我无聊得发疯
我讨厌我的伪装
那渴望的面具
但我能怎么办
没有伪装
我就无法被创造
我的救世主是个女人
她的照片没了
一百年前
我们抛弃了它
"给我们那位女士，"他们说。
"现在太危险了，
"墙上不能有她的肖像。"
于是我交出了她
连同她的语言
那快乐的语言
是她为了她的名而造
任何一个人

想要谈论她
就得变成像我一样
屈辱而沉默
为情所困
擅长于无聊
及其他孩子气的事

（孔亚雷　译）

MY REDEEMER

I think of you all the time
But I can't speak about you any more
I must love you secretly
I must come to you when I am alone
As I am now
And even now I must be careful
I want all the women
You created in your image
That is why I lower my eyes
When I pass them in the street
You can hear my prayer
The one I have no words for
The name that I cannot utter
I'm twisted with love
I'm burning with boredom
I hate my disguise
The mask of longing
But what can I do
Without my disguise

I wouldn't be created
My Redeemer is a woman
Her picture is lost
We surrendered it
A hundred years ago
"Give us the Lady," they said.
"It is too dangerous now
"to have her likeness on a wall."
So I gave her away
And the language with her
The happy language
She invented for her name
And anyone who wants
To talk about her
Has to become like me
Humiliated and silent
Twisted with love
A specialist in boredom
And other childish matters

起先

起先没事
过一阵
还是没事
夜里一家会路过
提醒孩子上床
那是你点烟
的信号
微妙时刻到了
一伙林区爷们儿
围着桌子
讨论你的生活方式
用一杯樱桃汁
解散他们
你的生活方式结束
很多年了
月光照耀的山
环绕你的心
那背包拄棍的
救世主
会在小路被认出
他或许正想
你百年前在校园
说过的话
这是危险时刻
会把你打入
永世的沉默
幸好有单簧管声

自流浪的克莱兹默*
乐队
飘入厨房
让你分心
从不快的冥想
冰箱将转入
二档
那猫会爬上
窗台
毫无缘由
你会哭起来
泪水会干
你渴望有伴侣
我会是伴侣
起先我们没事
而后来
我们又出事了

(北岛 译)

---

* 克莱兹默 (Klezmer) 是犹太人古老的民间音乐。

174

FIRST OF ALL

First of all nothing will happen
and a little later
nothing will happen again
A family will pass by in the night
speaking of the children's bedtime
That will be the signal
for you to light a cigarette
Then comes a delicate moment
when the backwoods men
gather around the table
to discuss your way of life
Dismiss them with a glass of
cherry juice
Your way of life has been over
for many years
The moonlit mountains
surround your heart
and the Anointed One
with his bag and stick
can be picked out on a path
He is probably thinking of what
you said
in the schoolyard 100 years ago
This is a dangerous moment
that can plunge you into silence
for a million years
Fortunately the sound of clarinets
from a wandering klezmer
ensemble
drifts into the kitchen
Allow it to distract you
from your cheerless meditation
The refrigerator will go into
second gear
and the cat will climb onto the
windowsill
For no reason at all
you will begin to cry
Then your tears will dry up
and you will ache for a companion
I will be that companion
At first nothing will happen to us
and later on
it will happen to us again

十字架

我是西奥多罗斯
一个不会读写的诗人
当我老得没法再干活
我就给旅游商店
做些宗教纪念品
我破门而入
把手伸向那些女人
那些美国和巴黎来的女人
就是她们
说我是个诗人
我不会向你诉苦
说我儿子的堕落
或我的海上生涯
我雕刻十字架
并跟所有其他人一样
身上带着一个

我的欲望让女人们吃惊
我给她们捕鱼
用鱼叉和潜水镜
我喂她们吃
她们从未吃过的东西
如果你是个女人
如果你顺着这个男人
功绩的刨花
你就会在月光下
看见我强壮的鬼影
从海路去维利裘斯*
如果你是个男人
你会在同一条路上
听见女人们的声音
正如我听到的那样
从水中传来

从船上传来
从船与船之间传来
然后想必
你就会理解我的人生
并通过宽恕我
来救助我的灵魂
为此我向他祈祷
向那个把我塑造成我的人

为此我在酒后
向伦纳德斯
我的希伯来朋友
忏悔
他把它写了下来
为那些后来人
　　　——卡米尼，海德拉岛，1980

---

* 维利裘斯（Vlychos）是希腊海德拉岛上的一处海滩名。

THE CROSS

I am Theodoros
the poet who could not read or write
When I was too old to work
I made religious items
for the tourist shops
I broke down doors
and I put my hands on women
women from America and Paris
They were the ones
who said that I was a poet
I will not tell you about my problems
my son's fall
or my life at sea
I carved crosses
and like everybody else
I carried one
I astonished women with my desire
I fished for them
with goggles and a spear
and I fed them
with what they had never eaten before
If you are a woman
and you follow the shavings
of this man's effort

in the moonlight
you will see my muscled ghost
on the sea road to Vlychos
and if you are a man
on the same road
you will hear women's voices
exactly as I heard them
coming from the water
coming from boats
and from in between the boats
and then surely
you will understand my life
and do a kindness to my soul
by forgiving me
I pray this to the one
who fashioned me out of myself
I confess this
over the wine
to Leonardos
my Hebrew friend
who writes it down
for those to come

— *Kamini, Hydra, 1980*

178

厌倦

　　我们已经厌倦了做白也厌倦了做黑，我们打算不再做白也不再做黑。我们现在打算做声音，做蓝天下灵魂出窍的声音，做你们忧愁洞里的悦耳和声。我们打算一直就这样，直到你们改邪归正，直到你们受的苦难让你们镇静下来，于是你们就能相信上帝说的话，他已经对你们说过那么多次，用各种方式，叫你们要爱彼此，或者至少，不要去杀人放火——以某种愚蠢的令人作呕的人类思想为名义，那会让上帝离你们而去，会让宇宙因难以想象的悲伤而一片昏暗。我们已经厌倦了做黑，我们打算不再做白也不再做黑。

TIRED

　　We're tired of being white and we're tired of being black, and we're not going to be white and we're not going to be black any longer. We're going to be voices now, disembodied voices in the blue sky, pleasant harmonies in the cavities of your distress. And we're going to stay this way until you straighten up, until your suffering makes you calm, and you can believe the word of G-d who has told you so many times, and in so many ways, to love one another, or at least not to torture and murder in the name of some stupid vomit-making human idea that makes G-d turn away from you, and darken the cosmos with inconceivable sorrow. We're tired of being black, and we're not going to be white and we're not going to be black any longer.

七十年代初即景*

　　总的来说，或者一般来说，正如你们所言，大众读者对多愁善感的小说没有兴趣是理所当然的。或者换个方式说，我跟你们大部分人很不一样，我越老，就越高兴。我本该像一个来自不同国家的人，用我祖国的恐怖来逗你们开心，但我没有。我恰恰来自你们当中，或者你可以说，来自你们的迷雾**。我就是你们的迷雾**。但不要惊慌；站在你面前的不是个话唠。如果我太容易把双关语搞得很深奥，那只是因为我已经受不了了。我磕了太多迷幻药，我太寂寞，或者我受的教育超过了我的智力水平，或者你想怎么解释都行。有那么一种想法，觉得以某种方式，他的声音，他的作品象征着深不可测的心海冰库里最深处，最难找，最新鲜也最天然的现实的牡蛎，如果有人非要用这种想法来抚慰自己被搞砸的生活，那真是遗憾。但你们也知道，我就是这样的人。令人惊讶的是，在那些真正理解我的一小群人中，我非常有名。我是痛苦之音，我无法被安慰。许多人曾经试过，但很显然，也很幸运，他们那寒酸的安慰对我毫无作用。在我无聊闲扯的巨网中，我会毫不费力地俘获你的眼泪。我打算告诉你这样一个爱情故事，它会让你庆幸你不是我，但谁知道呢，你也许会在欣喜后啜泣，正如我暗示过，甚至保证过的那样。我觉得那是个好故事。我觉得它很坚韧。我觉得它有纤维感。我跟许多人说过这个故事，他们都很喜欢。现在我打算把它告诉你。在我的资格证书中，其中有一项是黑照片的发明人。去问问地铁上某个消息灵通的上班族，他会不屑一顾地吼着说：哦，是的，就是那个家伙，费老大工夫取好景，然后拍的时候又拿手遮住镜头。这个假想旅客的话真把我给逗乐了，所以我干脆就用他的描述来说明我的艺术创作。我的艺术，我的不朽。当这种对人性怪诞拙劣的模仿逐渐发展成某种——毫无疑问——更糟的东西，我将成为未来眼球的焦点。未来的子孙后代，那些小恶魔，将会在我单调乏味的正方形所散发的艺术气息中流连忘返，度过许多美妙的假期。几年前一个聪明的纽约艺术商想利用我不朽艺术中最显而易见的方面来炒作一下，于是有几个月时间我成了第十大道上的一个人物，成了一个小圈子的宠儿，这个小圈子由一帮出奇瘦小的家伙组成，他们致力于推进一种叫艺术科学的"新"型人类表达方式。这帮狂热者中有人试图让我相信他们明白我在做什么。不用说，他们表错意了，就像神话中的亚当。人们关于黑照片所说的话没有一句对我有丝毫意义，当然，除了妮可***。她懂它们。她知道我在做什么。她知道我

180

是谁。我对她仍然充满渴望。我会在我最后几十年的无聊和琐碎经历中细心筛选，把我真正活着的——当然，在人的意义上——那一时期讲述给你听。从另一种意义上说，在希腊古瓷的国度里，在水晶和永恒钻石的历史上，我依然是"绝对的创造者"，对于我碰过的任何东西，我就是生命的源泉，就像一个女人的手放在少年胯下那样一触即发，那样不可抗拒，那样神魂颠倒确定无疑。我曾经是，现在也是，将来还是那个"造物主"****，那个"无生命体的救世主"。现在你大概对我在黑照片中自己构想的那种挑战精神有所感觉了吧。看着所有我那些可怜的狗屎——有些人会那样，也应该那样叫它——妮可立刻理解了我。在妮可的眼里，我的作品，跟其它玩意儿相比，是一座纪念碑。在我自己的时间里，有那样一双眼睛，我遇见了它们，脑门对着脑门；黑照片对着另一个人的虹膜歌唱，对了，还有眼角膜，视网膜和视觉神经，然后沿着脏皮包一直往下，对着妮可不安的心——另一个人的心——歌唱；当这真的发生了，对于我的孤独，不朽所造成的孤独，就成了致命一击，那就是她。

　　因此开幕时我在纽约，纽约的某个地方；事实上，那地方就是切尔西旅馆。那位聪明的艺术商，就叫他亚哈吧，对我有一种令人伤心的错误印象，认为我会很喜欢在那样一个肮脏的大堂里进进出出，那里堆挂着楼上工作室那些雄心勃勃的骗子制造的时髦排泄物：巨大的雪茄盒复制品；枕头般的帆布像许多啤酒肚一样鼓出无辜的画框；幼稚的电磁装置炫耀着艺术家对科技很在行；那些移动装置，做得如此糟糕，以致于它们的精神危害力与肉体杀伤力已经合二为一；各种大小的白兰地酒杯，漆成红色摆在一个玻璃橱柜里；它们全都以某种无聊的透视变化为由头，就像那就是人类所需要的；而且所有这些把戏，所有这些丑陋的动机，所有这愚人村式狡诈的毒药箱，都推销说自己是拯救这个垂死文化的紧急特效药；所有这些渎神的行为都在急剧膨胀；很快就在第二十三街及附近低垂的天幕下，堆积了一层又一层黏滞的沙砾；——预示着这些劣质宝贝转眼就会被不为人知地埋入时间之沙。那便是他让我住的旅馆。他以为我也是他们中的一员。迪伦·托马斯*****也从那个大堂游荡出来，他用眼睛去戳玫瑰刺，以便或以此，在挤满文弱英雄的万神殿里，去抢他应得的那张厚垫子的安乐椅。显而易见，我跟那个时代合不来。

　＊1966年科恩离开希腊来到纽约，开始了他的歌手生涯，并于1967年发行了自己的首张个人专辑，《莱昂纳德·科恩的歌》。本文用玩笑和比喻的方式，回忆了70年代初他在纽约的生活。

　＊＊原文中的midst（意为"在……当中"）和mist（意为"迷雾"）发音相近。

　＊＊＊妮可（Nico，1938—1988），原籍德国的歌手、模特及电影演员，曾多次出演安迪·沃霍尔导演的先锋电影，并曾担任"地下丝绒"乐队（Velvet Underground）的主唱，70年代初与科恩交往甚密。

　＊＊＊＊原文为"Ch---t of Matter"，Ch---t为Christ的改写。这是虔诚的犹太教徒的一种书写习惯，与将God改写为G-d的原因相同，都是为了避免上帝（God）或基督（Christ）之名被他人抹除或涂改。

　＊＊＊＊＊迪伦·托马斯(Dylan Thomas)，著名威尔士诗人，1953年猝死于纽约切尔西旅馆，据说他是因为把玫瑰刺入自己眼睛，引起并发症而导致死亡。

Something from the Early Seventies

By and all, or by and large, as you say, the reading public's disinterest in the novel of sensibility behooves itself very well. Or to put it differently, I am very different from most of you, and the older I get, the gladder. I should have come from a different country to entertain you with the horrors of my native land, but I didn't. I came from your very midst, or you could say, your very mist. I am your very mist. But don't be alarmed; you are not in the presence of a verbal fidget. If I strain too easily to push a pun into a profundity, it is only because I am at the end of my tether. I've taken too much acid, or I've been too lonely, or I've been educated beyond my intelligence, or however you want to explain me away. It's a pity if someone has to console himself for the wreck of his days with the notion that somehow his voice, his work embodies the deepest, most obscure, freshest, rawest oyster of reality in the unfathomable refrigerator of the heart's ocean, but I am such a one, and there you have it. It is really amazing how famous I am to those few who truly comprehend what I am about. I am the Voice of Suffering and I cannot be comforted. Many have tried but apparently, and mercifully, I am immune to their shabby consolations. I will capture your tear without hardly trying, in the vast net of my idle prattle. I am going to tell you such a love story that will make you happy because you are not me, but who knows, you may be sobbing behind your ecstasy, as I have hinted, or even promised. I think it's a good story. I think it's tough. I think it's got fibre. I've told it to a lot of people and they all liked it. I'm going to tell it to you. Among my credentials, I am the creator of the Black Photograph. Ask some informed commuter on the subway and he might growl scornfully: Oh yeah, he's the guy who takes a lot of trouble setting up a picture and then holds his hand over the lens when he snaps it. I am truly amused by this fictitious traveller's conversation and I will let his description stand for the process of my art. My art, my eternity. I will be the delight of future eyes when this grotesque parody of humanity has evolved into something no doubt, worse. These future monsters of the unborn seed will pass many excellent vacations of intensity immersed in the emanations of my colourless rectangles. A few years back a clever New York art dealer attempted to capitalize on the most obvious aspects of my eternity, and for a few months I was a figure on Tenth Street, and the darling of a small clique of curiously small and thin people, who were devoted to promoting a "new" form of human expression called ArtScience. Some of these fanatics tried to convince me that they understood what I was doing. Needless to say, they were barking, as was Adam of the fable, up the wrong tree. Nothing anyone has ever said about the Black Photograph has ever meant a fig to me, except, of course, for Nico. She could read them. She knew what I was doing. She knew who I was. And I long for her still. I will pick my way back through the boredom and irrelevance of the last few decades and tell you of a time when I was truly alive, in the human sense, of course. In the other sense, in the realm of the Grecian Urn, in the annals of crystal and imperishable diamond, I have remained the Absolute Creator, life itself to whatever I touched, as immediate, as irresistible, as wild and undeniable as a woman's hand on the adolescent groin. I have been, I am, and I will remain the Ch---t of Matter, and the Redeemer of the Inert. Now you may have an inkling of the spirit in which I conceived for myself the challenge of the Black Photograph. Nico perceived me immediately through all my pathetic bullshit, as some would, and should, call it. My work, among other things, is a monument to Nico's eyes. That there was such a pair in my own time, and that I met them, forehead to forehead; that the Black Photograph sang to other irises, and yes, corneas, retinas and optic nerves, all the way down the foul leather bag to Nico's restless heart, another human heart; that this actually happened constitutes the sole assault on my loneliness that the Eternal has ever made, and it was her.

Therefore I was in New York at a curtain time, in a certain place; actually it was The Chelsea Hotel. This clever art dealer, call him Ahab, possessed the sad misimpression that I would enjoy coming in and going out through a grimy lobby heaped and hung with the fashionable excrement of the ambitious hustlers in the studios above: enormous reproductions of cigar boxes; pillowlike canvases billowing over their innocent frames like so many beer bellies; infantile electromagnetic devices to advertise the artist's acquaintance with technology; mobiles, so badly constructed, that they compounded their capacity for psychic offence with a physical hazard; cognac snifters of various size, painted red and enclosed in a glass cabinet; all in the name of some dreary change of perspective, as if that's what humanity needs; and all these tricks, all these ugly motives, all this poisonous medicine chest of Gotham cunning, promoting itself as the urgent specific to a dying culture; all this profanity made flesh; quickly accumulating layer after layer of viscous grit generated on Twenty-Third Street, and in the low heavens of the neighbourhood; – a presage of the dirty treasure's soon-to-be-unnoticed burial under the sands of time. That's the hotel he put me in. He thought I was one of them. Also Dylan Thomas sailed out from that lobby to pierce his eye on a rose-thorn and hence or thence to assume his rightful overstuffed easy chair in the crowded pantheon of flabby heroism. It can be quickly divined I am no friend of the age.

We will all be airbrushed

we become
frail
and people
see us
naked
who are
forbidden
to see us
naked

25/1/03

我们都将被修饰　　赤身裸体
　　　　　　　　　他们本来
我们变得　　　　　不准
很虚弱　　　　　　看见我们
人们　　　　　　　赤身裸体
看着我们　　　　　　03/1/25

黄油杯

亲爱的，现在我有个黄油杯
形状做得像奶牛

BUTTER DISH

Darling, I now have a butter dish
that is shaped like a cow

争吵

你也许是个喜欢
跟永恒争吵的人。开始这样一场争吵
有个好办法：

> 为什么你要否定我
> 为什么你要我现在安静
> 什么时候我才能口出真理
> 额头发光？

经过一段时间之后，这些问题的答案
会从你的肚子里往上升，或者从你的帽顶上
往下漏，或者终于，药到病除，
你也许会开始爱上那个提问的人；
也有可能你会大喊大叫，就像我们许多父母那样：

> 上帝保佑你
> 让我的争吵
> 变得更甜

ARGUMENT

You might be a person who likes to
argue with Eternity. A good way to
begin such an Argument is:

Why do You rule against me
Why do You silence me now
When will the Truth be on my lips
And the Light be on my brow?

After some time has passed, the answer to these questions
percolating upwards from the pit of your stomach, or downwards
from the crown of your hat, or having been given, at last, the right
pill, you might begin to fall in love with the One who asked them;
and perhaps then you will cry out, as so many of our parents did:

Blessed be the One
Who has sweetened
my Argument.

很久以后

二十年前
在阳光下
雷·查尔斯唱着《你又赢了》
我永远都成不了他
而我年轻的妻子
"我年轻时的妻子"
在老屋
楼上的房间对我微笑
雷·查尔斯和玛丽安娜*
我希腊人生的亲爱灵魂
在每个新夏天的阳光下现身
玛丽安娜走下楼梯

"屋子的女主人"
雷·查尔斯在热烈宣扬
我们纯洁的人性
二十年前
和今年好莱坞的又一个夏天
他们依然是我
心的伴侣
当我再一次
拿我年轻时甜美的高标准
衡量自己

——洛杉矶，1978

---

*雷·查尔斯（Ray Charles），美国著名黑人爵士歌手，被称为"灵魂歌王"；玛丽安娜（Marianne），科恩年轻时在希腊的同居女友，他曾为她写过一首著名的歌曲，《再见，玛丽安娜》（So Long, Marianne）。

MUCH LATER

Ray Charles singing You Win Again
in the sunlight
twenty years ago
Ray Charles the singer I would never be
and my young wife
'the wife of my youth'
smiling at me from an upstairs room
in the old house
Ray Charles and Marianne
dear spirits of my Greek life
now in the sunshine of every new summer
Marianne coming down the steps
'the woman of the house'
Ray Charles speaking fiercely
for our virgin humanity
Twenty years ago
and again in this Hollywood summer
still companions of the heart
as I measure myself once more
against the high sweet standards
of my youth

> — *Los Angeles, 1978*

又一个克利斯托弗

又一个克利斯托弗*
被引向坎坷途
一路背负被抛弃的基督
你们的事他没法顾

ANOTHER CHRISTOPHER

There is another Christopher
Guide to Broken Ways
Rejected Christ he carries far
Yours he cannot raise

心心相印勋章　照准颁行

---

* 克利斯托弗（Christopher）是一个传说中的人物，又名圣克利斯托弗（Saint Christopher），为天主教十四救难圣人之一。据说他原名奥弗路斯（Offero），为了表示自己对上帝的虔诚，在一名隐士的建议下，他开始利用自己高大的身体背人过河。有一天，他背到一名沉重不堪的小孩，一问之下才知道他背的正是担负着全世界重责的基督。当下，基督以河水为奥弗路斯施浸礼，并将他改名为Christopher，意为"背负基督的人"（Christ-bearer）。

四分五裂

我不记得
我在做什么
我不记得
我这是站在哪儿
我在等人
但记得在等谁
我不记得
这是之前还是之后
突然或者渐渐
我被移到,被带到
这颠倒之地
我四分五裂
每个碎片所在之地
都有恐惧的名字
而在巨大的纪念碑上
刻着悲伤的名字
如果你知道怎样
为这般游离的人祈祷

请或读或唱,为他祈祷
你们这些
关心此类问题的善良人
如果在字里行间
有一点空隙
有一片可以回归的果园
请用只有你能控制的
声音或手
把我的名字牢牢安在那儿
但请快一点
因为那在我恳求之下
短暂聚合的碎片
又开始分离
散落到"另一边的世界"
那儿天使倒挂
一切都落满尘埃
人人都羞愧难当
而且谁也不准放声哭喊

SEPARATED

I was doing something
I don't remember what
I was standing in a place
I don't remember where
I was waiting for someone
but I don't remember who
It was before or it was after
I don't remember when
And suddenly or gradually
I was removed, I was taken
to this place of reversal
and I was separated
and in the place of every part
there was the name of fear
and for a vast memorial
there was the name of grief
If you know the prayer
for one who has been so dislocated

please say it or sing it
and if there is among the words
an empty space, or among the letters
an orchard of return
please set my name firmly there
with a voice or hand
which only you command
you righteous ones
who are concerned with such matters
But hurry please
for all the parts of me
that gathered briefly around this plea
are dispersed again
and scattered on the Other Side
where the angels stand upside down
and everything is covered with dust
and everyone burns with shame
and no one is allowed to cry out

ANGRY AT 11 PM

发火，晚上11点

you don't want to go out any more
it's bearable alone
just you and the bad news
and the confession of Mother Theresa
G-d Bless her for letting us know
that she couldn't take it either

2.18.03

你再也不想出门了
一个人还行
只剩你和那些坏消息
还有特丽莎修女的忏悔
上帝保佑她，她让我们知道
她也受不了了

03.2.18

第三项发明

我盲目地研制
    我的第三项发明
像个迷路的人
    四处碰着运气

我一路摸索
    想找个更干净的说法
关于我无意中发现的
    一个绝对的污秽

这全是为了
    一个感兴趣的女人
驾着夜晚的
    最后一丝光明

美女游客
    失望透顶
准备爱上
    一个幽灵

幽灵在此
    带着他的第三项发明
平常的垃圾
    却换来至高奖励

第三项发明
    准备就绪
准备爱上
    这个世界

当他后退
    她就前进
第三项发明

    测算着他们

她躺进了
    第三项发明的怀抱
他回到房间
    着手第四项发明

这项作品
    自命不凡到极点
是对世界
    自发的颂歌

哦，深深沉湎于
    忘情的工作
他迷失在第四项发明
    他迷失在第三项发明

——1980

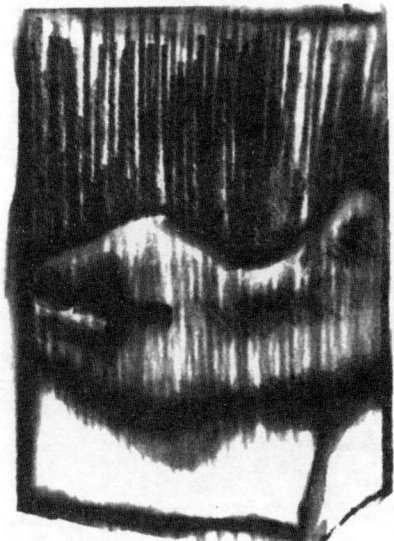

THE THIRD INVENTION

Blindly I worked
     at my third invention
taking the chances
     of one who is lost,

feeling my way
     to a cleaner expression
of the absolute filth
     I stumbled across.

And all for the sake
     of an interested woman
riding the night's
     last flicker of hope,

some tourist of beauty
     in full disappointment,
ready to fall in love
     with a ghost.

and here was the ghost
     with his third invention
the usual shit
     for the highest reward;

and now it was ready,

     the third invention,
ready to fall
     in love with the world.

And he falls back
     and she comes forward;
his third invention
     measures them both.
She lies in the arms
     of his third invention
and back in his room,
     he commences the fourth.

This is the work
     of the highest pretension
an automatic ode
     to the world.

O deep in the comfort
     of full employment,
he's lost to the fourth
     and he's lost to the third.

     – 1980

妈妈睡着了

回想起妈妈
在雅典的一家剧场
三十
三十五年前
塞奥多拉基斯的一出讽刺剧
那些美妙的歌
她睡着了
就在我旁边的位子
在一家露天剧场
她那天刚到
从蒙特利尔
而演出
快午夜才开始
她睡过了
曼陀林
不断攀高的和声
以及那些美妙的歌
我还年轻
还没有自己的孩子
我不知道你的爱
可以越过千山万水
我不知道
那会让你多么累

MY MOTHER ASLEEP

remembering my mother
at a theatre in Athens
thirty
thirty-five years ago
a revue by Theodorakis
those great songs
she fell asleep
in the chair beside mine
in the open-air theatre
she had arrived that day
from Montreal
and the play started
close to midnight
and she slept through
the mandolins
the climbing harmonies
and the great songs
I was young
I hadn't had my children
I didn't know how far away
your love could be
I didn't know
how tired you could get

又见罗伯特

好啊，罗伯特，你又在这儿，在巴黎的花神咖啡馆跟我聊天。我已经有阵子没见你了。你死后我写的那首十四行诗，写了好几个版本，但总觉得不对劲。我爱你，罗伯特，我仍然爱着你。你是个有趣的人，也是第一个真正和我争吵的朋友。吃了半片在这件旧外套里找到的安非他命*，我有点儿恍恍惚惚，这药放了大概已有二十年了，我就着橘子汁把它吞下去。过了这么久，它不可能还有药效，但你瞧，就在这儿，我们又聊上了。我很高兴你没告诉我你呆的地方是个什么样，因为我对来世不感兴趣。跟往常一样，你有点恼火，就像刚从什么极为无聊的事情中脱身。就这样，我们聊着我们替自己谈下的烂生意。你说什么？你为什么笑？我还在努力工作，罗伯特。我似乎已经没法把什么事情好好做完，我真的有麻烦了。安非他命的药效，或者说情绪，正在减弱，关于我的麻烦，我没法再跟你讲个好笑的故事，但你知道我什么意思。在所有朋友中，你最知道我。好吧，再见，罗伯特，你这个狗娘养的。你的非实体性赋予了你许多特权，但你应该为自己说声抱歉，谁知道这次你又要消失多久。

---

*安非他命（speed），一种致幻麻醉品。

ROBERT APPEARS AGAIN

Well, Robert, here you are again talking to me at the Café de Flore in Paris. I haven't seen you for a while. I have several versions of that sonnet I wrote after your death but I never got it right. I love you, Robert, I still do. You were an interesting man, and the first friend I really quarrelled with. I'm slightly stoned on half-a-tab of speed I found in this old suit, it must be twenty years old, and I took it with a glass of orange juice. It couldn't possibly work after all this time, but here we are, talking again. I'm glad you don't tell me what it's like where you are because I have no interest in the afterlife. You're a little pissed off as usual, as if you've just come from something immensely boring. Here we are, talking about the lousy deal we negotiated for ourselves. What are you saying? Why are you smiling? I'm still working hard, Robert. I can't seem to bring anything to completion and I'm in real trouble. The speed is wearing off, or the mood, and I can't tell you an amusing story about my trouble, but you know what I mean. Of all my friends you know what I mean. Well, goodbye, Robert, and fuck you too. Your disembodied status entitles you to a lot of privileges, but you might have excused yourself before disappearing again for who knows how long.

妈妈没有死

我妈妈没有真的死。
你的也是。
我真为你开心。
你以为妈妈死了，
而其实她没有。
那你父亲呢？
他好吗？
所有亲人你都不用担心。
看见那些昆虫了吗？
它们中有一只曾经是你的狗。
但别去拍蚂蚁。
它会被你笨拙的爱害死。
那棵树想要抚摸我。
它曾经是一个下午。
妈妈啊，妈妈
我终于不必再想念你。
鲁瓦，鲁瓦，瑞克斯，斯博特*，
这儿有我心的骨头。

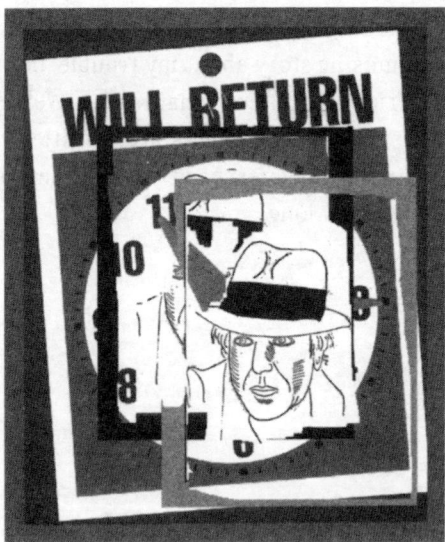

– after a photo by Hazel Field

---

* 鲁瓦，瑞克斯，斯博特是作者臆想的三只狗，这三个名字是美国六七十年代最常
见的狗名。

MY MOTHER IS NOT DEAD

My mother isn't really dead.
Neither is yours.
I'm so happy for you.
You thought your mother was dead,
And now she isn't.
What about your father?
Is he well?
Don't worry about any of your relatives.
Do you see the insects?
One of them was once your dog.
But do not try to pat the ant.
It will be destroyed by your awkward affection.
The tree is trying to touch me.
It used to be an afternoon.
Mother, mother,
I don't have to miss you any more.
Rover, Rover, Rex, Spot,
Here is the bone of my heart.

雪莉

让我回头从雪莉说起
她知道在火花
蹿起之前
我是怎么样的人
她领我到
袖口的自行车
在她面前
我是古希腊的
玻璃棒球
我母亲口中的
飞天石头
雪莉明白
我的草帽和口红
光洁的苏打式雄心
以及稍纵即逝的
灵光乍现

她是
蝙蝠窝里的
笑声保姆
她大笑
当我出乎意料地
降生在父亲的刮须盒
但够了你
你，还有你
你们这些
占据高位的家伙
我可是
有红色勋章的老兵
雪莉真正的朋友

回到你们那些
冬天的树叶
和伤感的
有关税收宝库的
笑话中

（孔亚雷　译）

SHIRLEY

Let me go back to Shirley
She knew who I was
before the ascension
of sparks
She led me to
the bicycle of armholes
and in her front
I was the glass baseball
of Ancient Greece
the soaring stones
of my mother's mouth
Shirley understood
my straw and my lipstick
the lacquered soda of ambition
and the splash of mind
as it all goes by

She was the

Nurse of Laughter
in the Bat-House
She laughed when
I was born as a surprise
in my father's shaving kit
But enough of you and
you and you
who have captured
all the High Places
I am the veteran
the badge of red
the very friend of Shirley
Return to your
leaves of winter
and your sad jokes
about the reservoirs of
taxation

最好

印度有最好的冰激凌
美国最好的巧克力
英国最好的男人腿
西班牙最好的十字架
意大利最好的雾
以色列最好的紧急状态
加拿大最好的光
墨西哥最好的鹰
葡萄牙最好的孤岛
埃及最好的少数民族
挪威最好的音乐
摩洛哥最好的犹太人
韩国最好的意大利饭
我去过太多国家
一离开蒙特利尔我就完了
我和无法理解的女人见面
我假装对食物感兴趣
完全是对雪的恐惧
完全是上帝的旨意
完全是那颗心
吞噬其他器官的
五个夏日
两个春日
主要是我的狗死了
悲伤从此开始
渴望是欢乐所在
而我无从开始
无从欢乐
我懒得敬神
书在四周打开

不管我阻挡
它们不断进入我房间
那有块楔形碑铭的
古老石板
当我住在蒙特利尔
我知道穿什么
我有旧衣服
和老朋友
我的狗死了
才十年或十五年
幸好没有空间
留给后悔
在沉思默想的
贫困中

（北岛　译）

THE BEST

India has the best Ice Cream
America the best Chocolate
England the best Male Legs
Spain the best Cross
Italy the best Mist
Israel the best Emergency
Canada the best Light
Mexico the best Eagles
Portugal the best Lonely Islands
Egypt the best Minorities
Norway the best Music
Morocco the best Jews
Korea the best Italian Food
I've been to too many countries
I died when I left Montreal
I met women I didn't understand
I pretended to get interested in food
But it was all The Fear of Snow
It was all The Will of G-d
It was all The Heart
swallowing The Other Organs
It was Five Days of Summer
and Two Days of Spring
Mostly it was the Death of my Dog
Sorrow is the time to begin
Longing is the place to rejoice
But I did not begin
and I did not rejoice
I was lazy in G-d
Books lie open all around me
Despite my efforts
they keep coming into my room
And there is a slab of old stone
with cuneiform inscriptions
When I lived in Montreal
I knew what to wear
I had old clothes
and old friends
and my dog had been dead
for only ten or fifteen years
Fortunately there is no Space
     for Regret
in The Poverty
of these Reflections

发条

乌鸦深知
在黄色长椅
坐在哪儿

波浪深知
从哪儿穿透

牢靠的
颌骨
完好装进
作家的头颅

未来人们
上发条般到来
在沉闷的
水泥拱门下

他们自己纳入
这实录的
午后

（北岛　译）

CLOCKWORK

the crow knows
exactly where to sit
on the yellow bench

the wave
exactly where to break

the jaw that will not
unclench
is fastened perfectly
to the writer's skull

future generations
come like clockwork
under the damp
cement arches

to include themselves
in this well-recorded
afternoon

醉鬼不分性别

今天早晨我又醒了过来
我要为此感谢主
世界就是一个猪圈
我必须戴上帽子

我热爱主我赞美主
我宽恕主
希望我不会遗憾
因为允许"他"存在

我知道你喜欢把我灌醉
对我说的话取笑一番
我很高兴你那样做
我每天都在渴望

我对天使很恼火
她拧了一下我大腿
使我爱上
每个经过的女人

我知道她们是你的姐妹
你的女儿老妈和老婆
如果我漏掉了哪个
那么我向你道歉

奔向天堂挺有意思
当你另辟蹊径
天主就是一只猴子
当你让"他"趴在背上*

天主就是一只猴子
同时也是一个女人
一片虚无之地
一副你的嘴脸

愿E**撞进你的太阳穴
再透过你的眼睛往外看
让你爱上
每个你鄙视的人

---

* monkey on one's back，直译为"猴子趴在背上"，意指有毒瘾。
** E在这里可能是指Ecstacy，即摇头丸，也可能是指口齿不清，把"He"——即
"他"，指天主——发成了"E"。

THE DRUNK IS GENDER-FREE

This morning I woke up again
I thank my Lord for that
The world is such a pigpen
That I have to wear a hat

I love the Lord I praise the Lord
I do the Lord forgive
I hope I won't be sorry
For allowing Him to live

I know you like to get me drunk
And laugh at what I say
I'm very happy that you do
I'm thirsty every day

I'm angry with the angel
Who pinched me on the thigh
And made me fall in love
With every woman passing by

I know they are your sisters
Your daughters mothers wives
If I have left a woman out
Then I apologize

It's fun to run to heaven
When you're off the beaten track
The Lord is such a monkey when
You've got Him on your back

The Lord is such a monkey
He's such a woman too
Such a place of nothing
Such a face of you

May E crash into your temple
And look out thru' your eyes
And make you fall in love
With everybody you despise

无所谓

打了败仗
签了条约
没被抓到
逃出生天

我必须抛弃
以往的生活
曾经有点名
但也无所谓

你们的胜利
如此彻底
于是你们有人
想要保留

我们这小小存在
的一份记录
我们穿的衣服
我们用的工具

我们士兵玩的
碰运气的游戏
我们切的宝石
我们写的歌曲

我们的和平法则
它的精髓是
丈夫领导
妻子指挥

以及所有这些
甜蜜的冷漠
那种表现
有人称之为爱

那甜蜜的冷漠
有人称为命运
但我们有
更亲密的称呼

多深刻的称呼
多真实的称呼
但它们于我已经失落
于你已经死去

没有必要
将其留存
有活着的存在
也有死掉的存在

有活着的存在
也有死掉的存在
我已经分不清
所以无所谓

我不会杀人
像你那样杀人
我不会仇恨
我试过但不行

没人能看懂　　　　　故事的讲述
那宏伟蓝图　　　　　有真实也有谎言
或谁将是　　　　　　你拥有这个世界
最后一个　　　　　　所以无所谓

NEVER MIND

The war was lost
The treaty signed
I was not caught
I crossed the line

I had to leave
My life behind
I had a name
But never mind

Your victory
Was so complete
That some among you
Thought to keep

A record of
Our little truth
The cloth we wove
The tools we used

The games of luck
Our soldiers played
The stones we cut
The songs we made

Our law of peace
Which understands
A husband leads
A wife commands

And all of this
Expressions of
The Sweet Indifference
Some call Love

The Sweet Indifference
Some call Fate
But we had Names
More intimate

Names so deep
and Names so true
They're lost to me
And dead to you

There is no need
That this survive
There's truth that lives
And truth that dies

There's truth that lives
And truth that dies
I don't know which
So never mind

I could not kill
The way you kill
I could not hate
I tried I failed

No man can see
The vast design
Or who will be
Last of his kind

The story's told
With facts and lies
You own the world
So never mind

有那么一刻

每天都有那么一刻，我跪倒在对你的爱面前。于是我又会记起，我还是那个男人。我知道，我毕生的事业就是做那样一个男人，伏在白色的石板书*上，在对你忠贞不渝、至高无上的爱中谦卑不已。现在是晚上八点二十七分。再一次，有关你的念头，把我从冷漠之谜中解救，

于是胸口中央
　　坚硬的轮子
变成了柔软的轮子

上帝在他的羔羊旁躺下
于是那些生灵
就有了勇气

他的王后
被一千个版本
她最宠爱的雄蜂
按摩着身体

而你在那儿
在我失去的厨房场景中
对着其他人微笑

而这便是我
完成工作的方式
直到又重新开始

---

*原文为tablet，可以指"药丸"，也可以指刻有经文的"石板书"，这里应该是指后者，用来比喻文中的"我"无比崇拜他的爱人，如同信仰宗教。

THERE IS A MOMENT

There is a moment in every day when I kneel before the love I have for you. Then I remember that I am still that man. And I know that my life's work is to be that man, who leans over a white tablet humbled in his constant and signifying love for you. It is eight twenty-seven in the evening. Once again the thought of you has rescued me from the puzzle of my indifference

and the hard wheel

in the chest's centre

becomes a soft wheel

G-d lies down next to His lamb

so the creature can

gather itself

His Queen is massaged

by a thousand versions

of Her most devoted drone

and there you are

smiling at someone else

in my vision of the lost kitchen

and that is the way

I finish my work

until it starts again

夜莺

我把屋子建在林边
这样我就能听见你歌唱
它很悦耳，它很美妙
爱全都开始绽放

祝你好运，我的夜莺，
很久以前我就发现了你
而今你那美丽的歌全已消失
森林将你关在中央

太阳在薄暮中落山
此刻你会将我呼唤
安睡吧，我的夜莺
在你的冬青枝条下

祝你好运，我的夜莺
我活着只为把你亲近
虽然你仍在某处歌唱
但我却再也无法聆听

NIGHTINGALE

I built my house beside the wood
So I could hear you singing
And it was sweet and it was good
And love was all beginning

Fare thee well my nightingale
'Twas long ago I found you
Now all your songs of beauty fail
The forest closes 'round you

The sun goes down behind a veil
'Tis now that you would call me
So rest in peace my nightingale
Beneath your branch of holly

Fare thee well my nightingale
I lived but to be near you
Though you are singing somewhere still
I can no longer hear you

不忠的妻子
仿洛尔迦诗作

夜色里的圣地亚哥
那天我刚好经过
我把她带到河边
是男人都会这么做

她说她还是处女
这跟我听说的可不一样
但我又不是宗教法庭
我就信了她说的话

是啊她完全是在撒谎
她有孩子和丈夫
你想要审判这个世界
但抱歉我可不想

灯火在我们身后熄灭
萤火虫脱掉了衣裳
破碎的人行道走到尽头
我抚摸着她沉睡的乳房

它们急切地向我开放
就像死而复生的百合
在一幅精美的刺绣背后
她的乳头隆起如面包

她的衬裙挺括，花里胡哨
在我们腿间被揉变了形
轰隆作响就像一朵活的云
被刀锋围攻

没有月光给树叶镀银
树变得狂野高耸
一队野狗在河滩巡逻
让夜生机勃勃

我们穿过荆棘和浆果丛
穿过芦苇和仙人掌
我在地上挖了一个坑
为她的湿头发做个窝

然后我解下我的领带
她脱掉她的裙装
我的皮带和手枪放在一旁
剩下的全都扯光

她的肌肤光滑如油膏
比贝壳还明亮
你的黄金和玻璃器皿
也从未那般闪耀

她的大腿从我身上滑落
就像受惊的鱼群
虽然我的大半生已被遗忘
但这我仍然记得

那夜我跑过了最好的大路
骑着一匹强悍的战马
但很快我就被颠翻
她成了驾驭的骑手

219

身为男人我不想重复
那些她大声说出的话语
再说我的嘴唇已被封住
从那时直到永远

很快每个吻里都开始有沙
很快黎明已准备就绪
很快夜晚就会
向黄水仙的弯刀投降

我送了她一件漂亮东西
我一直等到她展开笑颜
我可不是那种吉卜赛人
天生就会让女人伤心

我并没有坠入爱河。当然
这从来都不由你决定
但她来来回回地走动
而那夜我刚好经过

我把她带到河边
她披着处女的伪装
我把她带到河边
在夜色里的圣地亚哥

是啊她是在撒谎
她有孩子和丈夫
你天生就明辨是非
但抱歉我却不行

夜色里的圣地亚哥
那天我刚好经过
我把她带到河边
是男人都会这么做

THE FAITHLESS WIFE

after the poem by Lorca

The Night of Santiago
And I was passing through
So I took her to the river
As any man would do

She said she was a virgin
That wasn't what I'd heard
But I'm not the Inquisition
I took her at her word

And yes she lied about it all
Her children and her husband
You were meant to judge the world
Forgive me but I wasn't

The lights went out behind us
The fireflies undressed
The broken sidewalk ended
I touched her sleeping breasts

They opened to me urgently
Like lilies from the dead
Behind a fine embroidery
Her nipples rose like bread

Her petticoat was starched and loud
And crushed between our legs
It thundered like a living cloud
Beset by razor blades

No silver light to plate their leaves
The trees grew wild and high
A file of dogs patrolled the beach
To keep the night alive

We passed the thorns and berry bush
The reeds and prickly pear
I made a hollow in the earth
To nest her dampened hair

Then I took off my necktie
And she took off her dress
My belt and pistol set aside
We tore away the rest

Her skin was oil and ointments
And brighter than a shell
Your gold and glass appointments
Will never shine so well

Her thighs they slipped away from me
Like schools of startled fish
Though I've forgotten half my life
I still remember this

That night I ran the best of roads
Upon a mighty charger
But very soon I'm overthrown
And she's become the rider

Now as a man I won't repeat
The things she said aloud
Except for this my lips are sealed
Forever and for now

And soon there's sand in every kiss
And soon the dawn is ready
And soon the night surrenders
To a daffodil machete

I gave her something pretty
And I waited 'til she laughed
I wasn't born a gypsy
To make a woman sad

I didn't fall in love. Of course
It's never up to you
But she was walking back and forth
And I was passing through

When I took her to the river
In her virginal apparel

When I took her to the river
On the Night of Santiago

And yes she lied about her life
Her children and her husband
You were born to get it right
Forgive me but I wasn't

The Night of Santiago
And I was passing through
And I took her to the river
As any man would do

轻装旅行31号

我要轻装旅行
所以Au Revoir*
我会想念我的心
和我的吉他

这儿很美好
但太遥远
我已经无法
再多过一天

歌儿不会来了
但要是它们来
我就得回家
上帝保佑但愿不要

我猜我
只是已经
对你我
不抱希望

路上我遇见了
几个人
也在轻装旅行
我并不孤单

after a photo by Hazel Field

———————

*Au Revoir，法语，意为"再见了"。

TRAVELLING LIGHT #31

I'm travelling light
So Au Revoir
I'll miss my heart
And my guitar

It's lovely here
So far away
I couldn't take
Another day

The songs won't come
But if they did
I'd go back home
So G-d forbid

I guess I'm just
Somebody who
Has given up
On me and you

I'm not alone
I've met a few
Who were travelling
Travelling Light

后院

坐在花园里
跟我女儿的狗
看着橘子
和上面的天空

花影浮动
成双成对
倾听车流
听出新意

然后我开始
跟一首微弱的歌搏斗
它将把我打败
在离家千里之外

（孔亚雷　译）

BACKYARD

Sitting in the garden
With my daughter's dogs
Looking at the oranges
And the sky above

Flowers with their shadows
Moving two by two
Listening to the traffic
Hearing something new

Then I start to struggle
With a feeble song
Which will overcome me
Many miles from home

当我出去

当我出去告诉她
那不该说的爱
她躲进大理石主题
和黄金浮雕深处

当我活捉她
浮在她屁股上
她的胸怀是渔网
捕获婴儿嘴唇

她凝视中飘忽
我更加自由
得花点儿工夫
让我全透明

我找了好久
或许她想藏身
撕掉封皮撕掉书
故事散尽

线与雾造的人
留意她优雅之处
比我在其位
领略更多的美

（北岛　译）

WHEN I WENT OUT

When I went out to tell her
The love that can't be told
She hid in themes of marble
And deep reliefs of gold

When I caught her in the flesh
And floated on her hips
Her bosom was a fishing net
To harvest infant lips

A soft dismissal in her gaze
And I was more than free
But took a while to undertake
My full transparency

Ages since I went to look
Or she would think to hide
Torn the cover torn the book
The stories all untied

But someone made of thread and mist
Attends her every grace
Sees more beauty than I did
When I was in his place

vibrant,
but
dead

生气勃勃，
但已经
　　死了

目标

我不能离开房子
也不能接电话。
我的情绪再次低落
但我并不寂寞。

终于结清了
灵魂的账簿：
这个打了水漂，
那个全额支付。

至于说堕落，它
早已开始：
你无法阻止雨，
也无法阻止雪。

我坐在椅子上。
我看着街道。
对我失败的笑容，
邻居还以微笑。

我和树叶一起走路。
我和铬一起发亮。
我几乎还活着。
我几乎很舒服。

没人可追随
也没东西可教，
除了一点：目标
不可能达到。

THE GOAL

I can't leave my house
or answer the phone.
I'm going down again
but I'm not alone.

Settling at last
accounts of the soul:
this for the trash,
that paid in full.

As for the fall, it
began long ago:
Can't stop the rain,
Can't stop the snow.

I sit in my chair.
I look at the street.
The neighbour returns
my smile of defeat.

I move with the leaves.
I shine with the chrome.
I'm almost alive.
I'm almost at home.

No one to follow
and nothing to teach,
except that the goal
falls short of the reach.

正在写的作品

他将会病倒
然后孤独地死去

他是我一个小故事
里的主人公

故事名叫《祈祷山庄》

WORK IN PROGRESS

he's going to get sick
and die alone

he is the main character
in my little story called

The House of Prayer

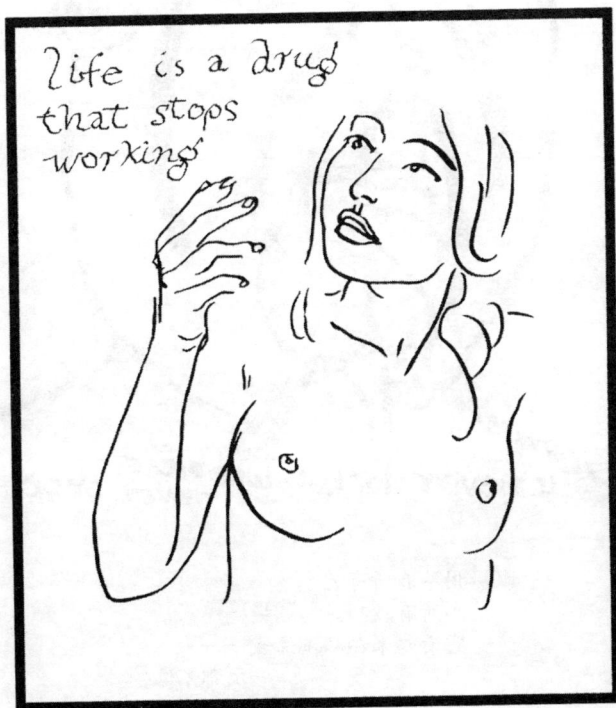

life is a drug
that stops
working

生命是一种
失效的
毒品

用尽我所有艺术
和所有技巧
它看起来却从不像我——
　　　　一次都不像

2003年9月15日

打开我的眼睛

今天早晨上帝打开我的眼睛
松开睡眠的绷带
让我看见
那个女侍者的小耳环
和她的小乳房
形成的两座小小山
又在餐厅的
双面镜里
让她的正面和背面叠加
赐予我速度
和多层次的观察
把我转得像个纺锤
这样我就能聚拢
并制作出
她所有版本的美
谢谢你世界的统治者
谢谢你叫我亲爱的

OPENED MY EYES

G-d opened my eyes this morning
loosened the bands of sleep
let me see
the waitress's tiny earrings
and the merest foothills
of her small breasts
multiplied her front and back
in the double mirrors
of the restaurant
granted to me speed
and the penetration of layers
and turned me like a spindle
so I could gather in
and make my own
every single version of her beauty
Thank You Ruler of the World
Thank You for calling me Honey

正确的态度

除了早上
在一位圣人陪伴下
度过的
那几个小时
其余时间
我都呆在床上
什么也不吃
只喝几口水
"你是个帅老头"
我对镜子里的自己说
"而且，更重要的是
你有正确的态度
你不在乎它会不会结束
或者它会不会继续
至于说女人
和音乐
天堂里
将来有的是"
然后我便去记忆的
清真寺
以表示我的感恩

THE CORRECT ATTITUDE

Except for a couple of hours
in the morning
which I passed in the company
of a sage
I stayed in bed
without food
only a few mouthfuls of water
"You are a fine-looking old man"
I said to myself in the mirror
"And what is more
you have the correct attitude
You don't care if it ends
or if it goes on
And as for the women
and the music
there will be plenty of that
in Paradise"
Then I went to the Mosque
of Memory
to express my gratitude

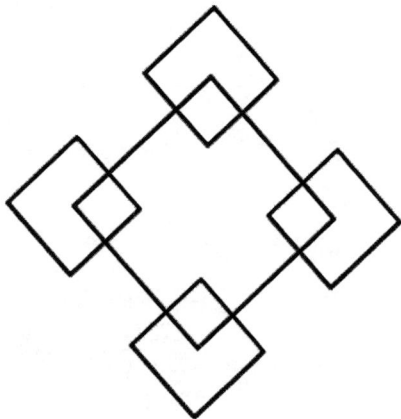

不是犹太人

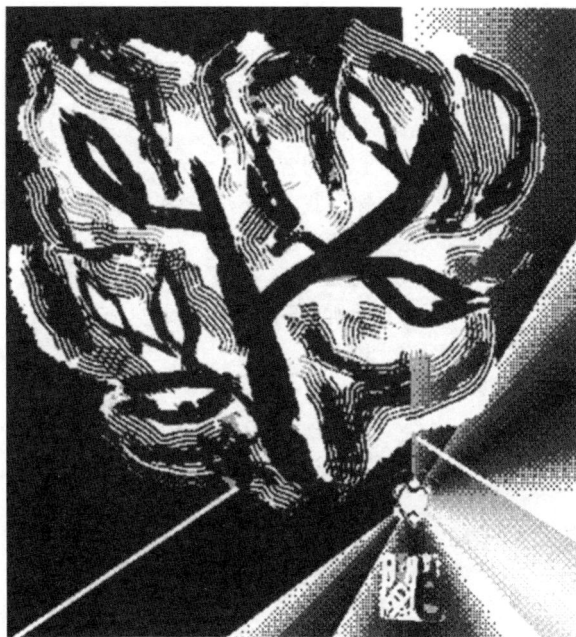

不管谁说
我不是犹太人
就不是犹太人
我很抱歉
但这是
最终裁决

NOT A JEW

Anyone who says
I'm not a Jew
is not a Jew
I'm very sorry
but this decision
is final

头衔

我有诗人的头衔
或许有一阵子
我是个诗人
我也被仁慈地授予
歌手的头衔
尽管
我几乎连音都唱不准
有好多年
我被大家当成和尚
我剃了光头，穿上僧袍
每天起得很早
我讨厌每个人
却装得很宽容
结果谁也没发现
我那大众情人的名声
是个笑话
它让我只能苦笑着
度过一万个
孤单的夜晚
从葡萄牙公园旁边
三楼的一扇窗户
我看着雪
下了一整天
一如往常
这儿一个人也没有
从来都没有
幸好
冬天的白噪音
消除了
内心的对话
也消除了
"我既不是思想，

智慧，
也不是内在的沉默之音……"
那么，敬爱的读者
你以什么名义
以谁的名义
来跟我一起
在这奢侈
每况愈下
无所事事的隐居王国中
闲逛?

TITLES

I had the title Poet
and maybe I was one
for a while
Also the title Singer
was kindly accorded me
even though
I could barely carry a tune
For many years
I was known as a Monk
I shaved my head and wore robes
and got up very early
I hated everyone
but I acted generously
and no one found me out
My reputation
as a Ladies' Man was a joke
It caused me to laugh bitterly
through the ten thousand nights
I spent alone
From a third-storey window
above the Parc du Portugal

I've watched the snow
come down all day
As usual
there's no one here
There never is
Mercifully
the inner conversation
is cancelled
by the white noise of winter
"I am neither the mind,
The intellect,
nor the silent voice within . . ."
is also cancelled
and now Gentle Reader
in what name
in whose name
do you come
to idle with me
in these luxurious
and dwindling realms
of Aimless Privacy?

木偶

德国木偶
烧死犹太人
犹太木偶
在劫难逃

木偶秃鹰
吞吃死人
木偶尸体
喂养它们

木偶风
木偶浪
木偶水手
在坟墓中

木偶花
木偶茎
木偶时间
拆除它们

木偶我
木偶你
德国木偶
犹太木偶

木偶总统
下达命令
木偶部队
燃烧土地

木偶炮火
木偶烈焰
吞噬所有
木偶名字

木偶情人
幸福无比
避而不见
所说一切

读者木偶
摇头晃脑
带着木偶
妻子上床

木偶黑夜
垂落下来
向木偶白昼
念收场白

（北岛　译）

238

PUPPETS

German puppets
burnt the Jews
Jewish puppets
did not choose

Puppet vultures
eat the dead
Puppet corpses
they are fed

Puppet winds and
puppet waves
Puppet sailors
in their graves

Puppet flower
Puppet stem
Puppet Time
dismantles them

Puppet me and
puppet you
Puppet German
Puppet Jew

Puppet presidents
command
puppet troops to
burn the land

Puppet fire
puppet flames
feed on all the
puppet names

Puppet lovers
in their bliss
turn away from
all of this

Puppet reader
shakes his head
takes his puppet
wife to bed

Puppet night
comes down to say
the epilogue to
puppet day

this mood has nothing to do with you

这情绪与你无关

一次也没有

印度到处都有
许多
超级美女
她们对我毫无欲望
这我每一天
都在证实
当我在孟买城里
走来走去
看着一张又一张面孔
一次也没有
例外

NEVER ONCE

India is filled
with many
exceptionally beautiful women
who don't desire me
I verify this
every single day
as I walk around
the city of Bombay
I look into face after face
and never once
have I been wrong

你到底记得谁

父亲死时我九岁；
母亲死时我四十六。
夹在中间，是我的狗和几个朋友。
最近，更多的朋友，
真正的朋友，
舅舅和婶婶，
好多熟人。
然后还有希拉。
她说，别做傻蛋，莱恩。
认真对待你的欲望。
她死的时候
我们刚过十五。

WHO DO YOU REALLY REMEMBER

My father died when I was nine;
my mother when I was forty-six.
In between, my dog and several friends.
Recently, more friends,
real friends,
uncles and aunts,
many acquaintances.
And then there's Sheila.
She said, Don't be a jerk, Len.
Take your desire seriously.
She died not long after
we were fifteen.

This is the best way to do it
We will be able to write like this
for a long long time
I think you will be able to read it
In fact, I'm sure you will
It will have pictures of me

in colour

这样做是最好的办法
我们可以像这样写
很长很长时间
我想你将会读到它
事实上，我确信你会
那上面将会有我的照片
彩色的

不看你

你看着我
而我从未想过
你也许正在挑选
这辈子的男人

你看着我
越过酒瓶和尸体
于是我想
你一定在玩我

你一定以为我会疯狂到
跟随你的眼光
走进打开的电梯

所以我不看你

所以我等待
直到你变成一棵棕榈树
或者一只乌鸦

或者巨大灰色的风的海洋
或者巨大灰色的心的海洋

现在你看我
娶谁也不会娶你

LOOKING AWAY

you would look at me
and it never occurred to me
that you might be choosing
the man of your life

you would look at me
over the bottles and the corpses
and I thought
you must be playing with me

you must think I'm crazy enough
to step behind your eyes
into the open elevator shaft

so I looked away
and I waited
until you became a palm tree

or a crow

or the vast grey ocean of wind
or the vast grey ocean of mind

now look at me
married to everyone but you

甚至我自己的几首

这是一切的尽头
不会再有更多
也许当我最后一次
站在舞台
从剧场最后排的楼座
会传来一两声叫喊
与此同时
用公认的好歌
给心做手术
比如《圣母颂》
和《希伯来祷歌》
甚至我自己的几首
并执行
推荐的仪式

比如跪在
一堆数量惊人的
日夜旁边
并把最新的分秒
拍到上面
就好像它是
一个孩子的沙堡
在一轮满月下
面对潮水，如此等等
也就是说
在老年忏悔者身上
激起
一种无边的展望

EVEN SOME OF MY OWN

This is the end of it all
There won't be much more
Maybe a cry or two
From the peanut gallery
Where I have made
My last stand
In the meantime
Operate on the heart
With proven songs
Such as Ave Marie
And Kol Nidre
Even some of my own
And execute
The recommended procedures

Such as kneeling down
Beside the appalling heap
Of days and nights
And patting the newest seconds
On to it
As if it were
A child's sandcastle
Facing the tide
Under a full moon etc.
In other words
Encouraging
In the old penitent
A borderless perspective

oh and one more thing
you aren't going to like
what comes after America

哦，还有件事
你可不能喜欢
跟着美国学的东西

248

你的心

我说了真话
结果你看怎么样
我本该写写
多伦多地下的
秘密河流
以及教师俱乐部的
审判
但我没有
我从一个人的胸口
扯出一颗心
并让每个人看
刻在上面
上帝的名字
很遗憾
那是
你的心
而不是我的
我没有值得一读的心
但我有刀
和神殿
哦,我的爱
难道你不知道我们已经被杀死
我们已经一同死去

YOUR HEART

I told the truth
and look where it got me
I should have written about
the secret rivers
under Toronto
and the trials
of the Faculty Club
but no
I pulled the heart
out of a breast
and showed to everyone
the names of G-d
engraved upon it
I'm sorry it was
your heart
and not mine
I had no heart worth the reading
but I had the knife
and the temple
O my love
don't you know that we have been killed
and that we died together

是什么困扰我

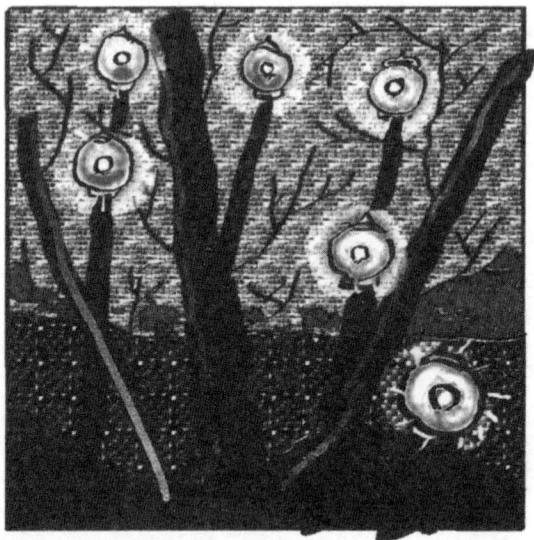

我为我的回忆而服药
但我还是无法阻止
它的消逝
我曾经有家人
他们能在水上行走
有根单向的锁链
把我拴在一个女人身上
她不知道她在前后左右地
将我猛扯
但她是谁
他们是谁?
就在某人
向我解释的时候
我忘了
是什么困扰我

WHAT BAFFLED ME

I took pills for my memory
but I could not stop it
from erasing
I had a family once
They could walk on water
There was a one-way chain
that held me to a woman's body
She didn't know she jerked me
every-which-way
But who was she
and who were they?
In the midst of
someone's explanation
I forget
what baffled me

风动

风吹动
棕榈树
和遮阳伞的
布边
孩子们滑下
水上滑梯
灰色的阿拉伯海
在污秽的海滩上
拍打着它穿脏的蕾丝内衣
风吹动一切
又停歇
但我的笔
继续
自动在写
亲爱的老师
我现在死了
我死在您前面
正如70年代初
您预言的那样

THE WIND MOVES

The wind moves
the palm trees
and the fringes
of the beach umbrellas
The children go down
the waterslide
The grey Arabian Sea
slaps its soiled lace underwear
on the dirty flats
The wind moves everything
and then stops
but my pen
keeps on writing
by itself
Dear Roshi
I am dead now
I died before you
just as you predicted
in the early 70s

老人的悲哀

老人和蔼。
年轻人愤怒。
爱也许盲目。
但欲望却不。

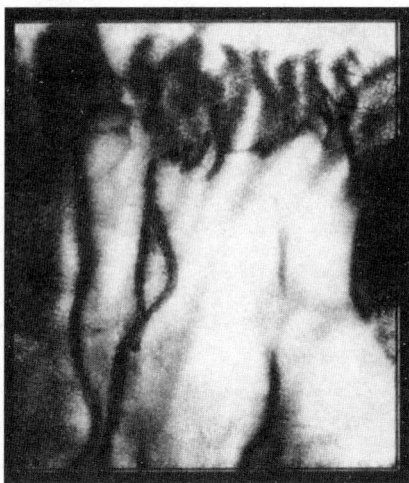

SORROWS OF THE ELDERLY

The old are kind.
The young are hot.
Love may be blind.
Desire is not.

back in
Montreal

as for the
past

Children
roshi
songs
Greece
Los Angeles

what
was that
all about?

November
18th
2003

回到\蒙特利尔\至于\过去\孩子\老师\歌\希腊\洛
杉矶\那一切\到底\是怎么回事?

2003年11月18日

终于孤独

最后
几百个早晨的
百忧解*
是多么苦

ALONE AT LAST

How bitter were
the Prozac pills
of the last
few hundred mornings

心心相印勋章

---

* 百忧解（Prozac），一种抗忧郁药。

254

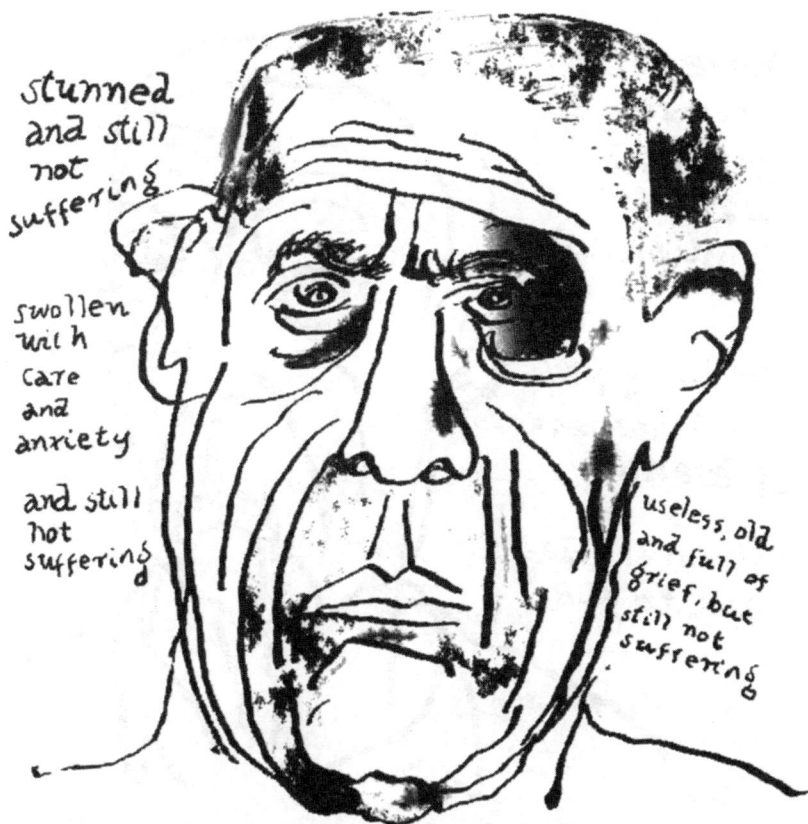

目瞪口呆\但还是\不\难受

满脑子\担心\和\忧虑
但还是\不\难受

又老又没用\充满\悲伤，但\还是不\难受

taxes
children
lost pussy
war
constipation

the living poet
in his harness
of beauty

offers the day
back to g-d

税收\孩子\失去的妞\战争\便秘
活着的诗人\戴着他美丽的\马具
把日子\还给上帝

相关

与此相关的任何东西，哪怕间接相关，都非常离谱。你们将会发现，无关联性就像有拯救力的肌肉，但用到和活动它的机会少之又少。必须承认绝望经济确实存在。我们并非老是需要艺术。时不时地让"她"脱下内衣。一点点就很有用。

目前，要看清"全局"（或"全猪"）只能通过松散的真经（或真菌），漂游的分子，和致癌物质。我死之后，回归经典。*我的理智是一种传染病。

虽然我们已经很多分钟没抽烟了，我们还是忍不住问酒吧服务员从他那包里讨了一根。

靠在巨大的厚玻璃窗上放松一下，让我们专注于由此而来的晕眩吧，全靠这些玻璃窗，我们才不会一头栽进12层楼高的孟加拉湾。

——泰姬陵酒店

---

*"我死之后"在原文中为法语Après moi，出自法国一句著名的谚语"Après moi, le déluge"，传为法国国王路易十五所说，意思是"我死之后，洪水滔天"，但常被曲解为"我死之后，哪管洪水滔天"。

ANYTHING WHICH REFERS

Anything which refers to the matter, even obliquely, is far from the mark. An incapacity for relevance is to be discovered as the muscle of salvation, but flexed and exercised as rarely as possible. The economy of desperation must be recognized. We don't need Art that often. Now and then let Her step out of Her underwear. A little goes a long way.

For the moment, the Big Picture (or the Pig Bicture) can be accessed only by means of the Loose Canon (or the Coose Lanon), the Drifting Molecule, the Carcinogenic Radical. Après moi, the return to Classical Proportion. My sanity is a contagion.

Although we have not smoked for many a minute, we are tempted to ask the barman for one from his own pack.

Let us concentrate on the vertigo produced by easing up to the great plate-glass windows, which are all that prevent us from plunging 12 storeys into the Bay of Bengal.

– The Taj Mahal Hotel

亚娜想着约翰

亚娜走出她的房子。几乎什么也没穿。手上还拿着杯子。她忘了把它放到桌上。寒冷让她想起自己忘了在内衣和衬裙外面套件衣服。她往回走。瑟瑟发抖。妈的，妈的约翰。

她不知道上帝已经把她杀了，还有约翰，还有她的波斯人泰芮，以及在下我，我比约翰或泰瑞爱她爱得更强烈，仅仅因为她是个女人。她不知道上帝已经把所有人都杀了。

亚娜曾经和我在一起。她更年轻的时候。她正在用老人做实验的时候。我想要了解你的身体，自闲。哦，没问题。这太怪异了，亚娜，身上没有内衣。可当她走回她没上锁的房间，她没叫我的名字。

杀我，我理解。杀约翰，我理解。杀亚娜，我理解，虽然我痛恨失去一个裸体女人。但泰芮，为什么上帝刚把泰芮想象出来，就把她杀了呢?

我是被放进亚娜里面的那些东西之一。一旦你被放进去了，你就被永远放进去了。那就是爱。有时它比死亡大，有时比死亡小，有时一样大。

约翰已经被杀了，但那并不是他的名字她说不出口的原因。那是因为对他的需要把她给弄散架了。那曾经是某种爱，但如今在巨大的痛苦和混乱中，那已经超越了爱的范畴。她已经完全忘了自己已经被杀。对于这种状况，除非你经历过，否则不要妄加评论。

不管怎样，生命继续。亚娜想着约翰，而不是我。他带她去停赛车的车库，让她猜哪辆是他的。她穿着一件白毛衣，买那件毛衣时她还是个意大利人。（米兰。墨索里尼的火车站。那些亲切的，被草汁染绿的女人，我再也没见过。我们都被来来往往的美丽潮水给杀了。）他们接吻。他得手了。她就像他法拉利赛车的凹背皮座椅那样令他销魂。

而在此，我的命运之神在我耳边低语："总有一天，在你的怀抱里，她将会明白自己一事无成。于是她就会被杀掉。许多像她那样的女人会来到你身边。有许多已经来了。你有一项工作。你有任务在身，而且你已经被杀了，连同整个理发店一道，不费吹灰之力。"

JANA THINKS OF JOHN

Jana comes out of her house. Wearing almost nothing. The cup is still in her hand. She forgot to leave it on the table. The cold reminds her that she has neglected to dress beyond her underwear and her slip. She turns back. Shivering. Damn you, damn you, John.

She doesn't know G-d has already killed her, and John, and Teri her Persian, and yours truly, who loves her more fiercely than John or Teri, merely because she is a woman. She doesn't know that G-d has killed everyone.

Jana was with me once. When she was younger. When she was experimenting with the old. I want to get to know your body, Jikan. Oh sure. This is sufficiently grotesque, Jana, without my undressing. But she doesn't call out my name as she returns to her unlocked door.

Me, I understand. John, I understand. Jana, I understand, although I hate to lose a naked woman. But Teri, why was Teri killed, as soon as G-d imagined her?

I was one of the things that was put into Jana. Once you have been put in, you have been put in forever. That is love. Sometimes it is greater than Death, sometimes smaller, sometimes the same size.

John has been killed, but that is not why his name is in her throat. It is because she is dismantled in her need of him. It used to be some kind of love but now it is beyond that in the magnitude of pain and dislocation. She has utterly forgotten that she has been killed. Do not comment on this condition unless you've been there.

Still, life goes on. Jana thinks of John, not me. He takes her out to the racing car garage, and she guesses which is his. She is wearing a white sweater which she bought when she was an Italian. (Milan. Mussolini's train station. Kind, grass-stained women I never saw again. All of us killed under the tidal beauty of coming and going.) They kiss. He is off the hook. Her essence is the very leatherness of the bucket seats of his Ferrari.

And over here, my destiny whispers, "Someday in your arms, she will come to understand that she never did anything. And then she will be killed. Many like her will come to you. Many have already come. You have a job. You are a man-at-work, and you have been killed, along with the whole barber-shop, without a hitch."

我的时间

我的时间快用完了
但我
还是没唱出
真正的歌
伟大的歌

我承认
我好像
已经失去了勇气

镜子里的一瞥
朝心里看一眼
都让我想
永远地闭嘴

所以，为什么你还让我在这儿
我生命中的主
让我靠在这桌边
在三更半夜
考虑
怎样才美

Room 215
Kemps Corner Hotel

肯普斯角旅馆
215房间

MY TIME

My time is running out
and still
I have not sung
the true song
the great song

I admit
that I seem
to have lost my courage

a glance at the mirror
a glimpse into my heart
makes me want
to shut up forever

so why do you lean me here
Lord of my life
lean me at this table
in the middle of the night
wondering
how to be beautiful

翻阅我的梦

我在翻阅我的梦
当我看见自己
在翻阅我的梦时
在翻阅我的梦
如此反复不已
直到在这
膨胀与收缩的
神秘活动中
我被耗尽
呼气与吸气同时进行
而后在我自个儿的屁眼里
自然消失
我已经这样干了三十年
但为了让你明白这感觉有多糟
我还在不停继续
如今我已到了一首歌的结尾
一次祈祷的尽头
一切都已灰飞烟灭
那是命中注定
锁链跟随着锚
缓缓地
沉入海底
这只是一首歌
只是一次祈祷
谢谢老师
谢谢大家

LOOKING THROUGH MY DREAMS

I was looking through my dreams
when I saw myself
looking through my dreams
looking through my dreams
and so on and so forth
until I was consumed
in the mysterious activity
of expansion and contraction
breathing in and out at the same time
and disappearing naturally
up my own asshole
I did this for 30 years
but I kept coming back
to let you know how bad it felt
Now I'm here at the end of the song
the end of the prayer
The ashes have fallen away at last
exactly as they're supposed to do
The chains have slowly
followed the anchors
to the bottom of the sea
It's merely a song
merely a prayer
Thank you, Teachers
Thank you, Everyone

你也一样

　　因为你很美，但闻起来很臭，所以我知道你已经被杀了。你对我也有同样的感觉。你说："你是位优雅的老人，但臭烘烘的。"在漫长的裸体交涉活动之后，你双手合十垂首。"谢谢，"你说，"这是我第一次什么也没做。"关于我的幸运，我听过许多动人的话，但无疑这是其中最动人的。"我现在闻起来怎么样？"我问。"比以前更糟。"你说。"我对你的感觉完全一样。"我说。随后你就回法国了（还是荷兰？），至今我们还是很铁的朋友。偶尔，当蜂鸟静止不动的时候，越过半个地球我都能闻到你腐烂的气息。

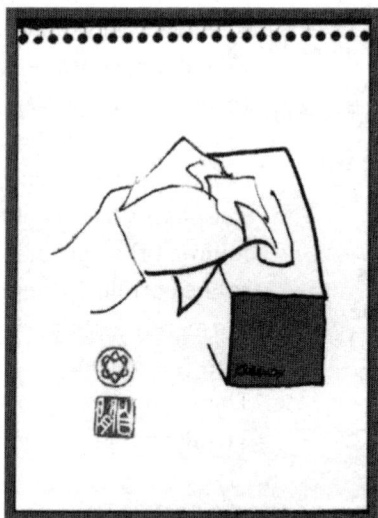

SO DO YOU

Because you are beautiful, but smelled bad, I knew you had been killed. And you felt the same about me. You said, "You are an elegant old man, but you stink." After the long event of naked intervention, you brought your hands together and bowed. "Thank you," you said. "That was the first time I never did anything." Many are the lovely things I have been told about my luck, but this was surely the loveliest. "How do I smell now?" I asked. "Worse than ever," you said. "Exactly my impression about you," I said. Then you went back to France (or was it Holland?) and we have remained fast friends ever since. Sometimes, when the hummingbirds are still, I can smell you rotting halfway across the world.

此刻，在我的房间

哦，我的爱
我又找到你了
我出门
买包香烟
而你就在那儿
我向每个人鞠躬
他们都为我开心
在爱你的
那只狗眼里
我迷失了自我
热气把我升了起来
堵车把我弹回床上
光着身子
旁边是一本关于你的书
和一瓶冷水

NOW IN MY ROOM

O my Love
I found You again
I went out
for a pack of cigarettes
and there You were
I bowed to everyone
and they rejoiced with me
I lost myself
in the eyes of a dog
who loved You
The heat lifted me up
The traffic bounced me
naked into bed
with a book about You
and a bottle of cold water

黑暗进入

黑暗进入我的旅馆房间
就像一面窗帘穿过另一面窗帘
翻滚成形状各异的黑暗
这儿是对翅膀，那儿是防毒面具
简单的东西，重叠的东西
我起身坐在床沿
用我的多重人格
阻挡黑暗的降临
正如一道顶端被漆成金色的
高高的尖顶栅栏
在阻挠法国的雨
一些明亮的时候
双方会打个平手
常常，在我一成不变的生活中

这高度紧张的片刻
一个女人会用万能钥匙进入房间
并简洁地想要说明
换成别的情况
我们本来可以生活在一起
我尤其喜欢
她用一种熟悉的方式
对我说着听不懂的语言
但每次在我心底
我都知道，重要的时刻
即将来临
而我就是那尖顶漆成金色的
高高的金属栅栏
在抵抗着必然

THE DARKNESS ENTERS

The darkness enters my hotel room
like a curtain coming through a curtain
billowing into different shapes of darkness
wings here a gas mask there,
simple things and double things
I sit upright on the edge of the bed
and I impede the falling darkness
with my many personalities
just as a high spiked fence
with the tips painted gold
interferes with the French rain
For a number of luminous hours
it is a standoff
Often during this highly charged segment
of my usually monotonous life
a woman enters the room with a pass-key
and in small ways manages to communicate
that we might have lived our lives together
had circumstances been otherwise
I like it especially
when she addresses me in the familiar form
of her incomprehensible language
but always in the back of my mind
I know the important moments
are on their way
and I am that high iron fence
with the spikes painted gold
holding off the inevitable

暗示

　　"我们是安大略来的女大学生。"

　　"安大略的什么地方？"

　　"我们对安大略不熟。有人告诉我们要这么说。"

　　"我明白了。"

　　她们故意在厨房里走来走去，打开又熄灭瓦斯炉，检查点火器，从塞满的橱柜里取出锅碗，跪在蔬菜保鲜盒面前，但并没有吃的真正做好端上来。

　　"其实我们不会做饭。"

　　"我知道。"

　　"其实我们只是一些暗示。我们的身体就是衣服。衣服下面什么都没有。"

　　"我正纳闷呢。"

　　"是啊，有人告诉我们要举止得体，要让你开心，让你微笑，不要让液体和裸体把你弄糊涂了。"

　　"这会让今晚好过一点吗？"

　　"会啊。这会让你感到快乐。"

　　"你们的好意我心领了。"

　　她们各自挽起他的手臂，依偎在他怀里，把头靠在他的胸前。

　　"我们爱你。"

　　他的眼泪流下来，她们用颜色鲜艳的丝巾替他擦去眼泪。

　　"我饿了。"

　　"我们也是！我们去蒙特利尔找家餐厅吧，那是座城市，我们听说，那儿每个街区的餐厅都比整个里约*还要多。我们每晚都出去吃，除非你不想出去。那我们就叫外卖。"

---

* 里约（Rio），里约热内卢（Rio de Janeiro）的简称，巴西原首都和第二大城市。

SUGGESTIONS

"We are college girls from Ontario."

"What part of Ontario?"

"We don't know Ontario. We were told to say we were from there."

"I see."

They moved purposefully around the kitchen, lighting and extinguishing the gas range, checking the pilot lights, extracting pots from crowded cabinets, kneeling in front of the crisper, but no food was actually cooked or served.

"We don't really know how to cook."

"I see."

"We are really nothing but suggestions. Our bodies end where our clothes begin. There's nothing underneath."

"I was wondering about that."

"Yes, we were told to practise modesty, to make you laugh and smile, and not to bewilder you with fluids and nakedness."

"Will this improve the evening?"

"It will. It will delight you."

"I submit myself to your good intentions."

They each took one of his arms, and they folded themselves against him, and pressed their heads against his chest.

"We love you."

His tears came and they wiped them away with their colourful bandanas.

"I'm hungry."

"So are we! Let's go to a restaurant in Montreal, a city, we have heard, which has more restaurants per block than even Rio. We'll go out every night, except when you don't feel like it. Then we'll order in."

Jikan
who pretended
to be a poet
breaks his pen

假装是个诗人\自闲\折断了他的笔

甚至现在

我不知道
你是那么单纯
那么慷慨
我想要征服你
用诗文
和色情的
暗示

甚至现在
你就在我心里
　　打着哈欠
无聊而寂寞
用油膏
涂遍全身
然后抚摸自己
我却还在徘徊

EVEN NOW

I did not know
how simple you are
how generous
I tried to capture you
with rhymes
and erotic
suggestions

Even now
you yawn
　　　in my heart
bored and alone
rubbing ointments
all over your body
and touching yourself
while I tarry

别的诗人

别的诗人一定会说
我多么爱你
但我现在太忙，忙着阿拉伯海
及它那白与灰的
固执重复

我已经厌倦了跟你说话
还有树
还有那些折叠躺椅

是啊，我在最后时刻
放弃了许多东西
包括说我爱你
这莫大的荣幸

我重新变瘦，变得英俊
我刮掉了祖父的络腮胡
我的腰带变松
我的下巴变紧

那些疯狂的年轻美女
身上还沾着灵修院
与神殿的尘垢
在一个老人的房间
考察她们的想象力

男孩们追随我的脚步
改变了他们的人生

在我催眠般的冷漠中
急切地探究
难以捉摸的现实

鲸鱼的脑袋
破浪而出
就像耀眼的落日
但我却只能看见
你或者"你"*
或者"你"中的你
或者你中的"你"

对其他人来说，这莫名其妙
但对于我
这完全是工作

我把年轻人
介绍给年轻人
他们在不幸中跳着舞离开
而我在
与阿拉伯海密谋
制造一种
丑陋的寂静
让大海
别再来烦我
更重要的是
让别的诗人去说
我多么爱你

_____

*作者在诗中用大写的You来指神或上帝，译文则用加引号的"你"表示。

275

ANOTHER POET

Another poet will have to say
how much I love you
I'm too busy now with the Arabian Sea
and its perverse repetitions
of white and grey

I'm tired of telling you
and so are the trees
and so are the deck chairs

Yes, I have given up a lot of things
in the last few minutes
including the great honour
of saying I love you

I've become thin and beautiful again
I shaved off my grandfather's beard
I'm loose in the belt
and tight in the jowl

Crazy young beauties
still covered with the grime
of ashrams and shrines
examine their imagination
in an old man's room

Boys change their lives
in the wake of my gait
anxious to study
elusive realities
under my hypnotic indifference

The brain of the whale
crowns the edge of the water
like a lurid sunset
but all I ever see
is you or You
or you in You
or You in you

Confusing to everyone else
but to me
total employment

I introduce
the young to the young
They dance away in misery
while I conspire
with the Arabian Sea
to create
an ugly silence
which gets the ocean
off my back
and more important
lets another poet say
how much I love you

原谅我

原谅我，先生们女士们，
如果我不认为自己
是一种病。
原谅我，如果我得到了圣灵
却没跟你们说。
原谅我，
西方的政委们，
如果你们觉得
我吃的苦还不够。

PARDON ME

Pardon me, lords and ladies,
if I do not think of myself
as the disease.
Pardon me if I receive the Holy Spirit
without telling you about it.
Pardon me,
Commissars of the West,
if you do not think
I have suffered enough.

她的朋友

她不知道
她的朋友来了

她无法
记下
他说的任何话

她的笔记本里
没有他的位置
不像卡比尔*
和南传上座部**

多年之后
她会想起
照看过一个老人

他们之间的
思想
有种好奇的赤裸

那种赤裸
那种透明
将带她回家

---

* 卡比尔（Kabir），1398年生于印度，圆寂于1518年，活了120岁。他是印度教的圣人，锡克教的上师，也是伊斯兰教的先知。他留下了两千多首诗歌和一千五百首对句。
** 南传上座部（Theravadins），指由印度本土向南传到斯里兰卡、缅甸等地而形成的佛教体系，在地理位置上处于印度之南，故称"南传佛教"。

HER FRIEND

she doesn't know
her friend has come

she won't be able
to write down
anything he says

he won't have a place
in her notebook
along with Kabir
and the Theravadins

many years later
she will remember
sitting with an old man

a curious nakedness
of thought
between them

that nakedness
that transparency
will lead her home

I guess it's better to start a war
or to stab a rabbi
than to look at yourself
in the mirror of your hotel room
It's better to get carried away
by your culture
    the brave children
    in front of the tanks
    the holy soil
        speaking your language
Shame on you, Great Poets!
I love the past as well as you
but I've got to do something
 to change your stupid bloodthirsty
        music
which no one but G-d really likes
GET BACK TO YOUR DIARIES

我猜就算开始打仗
或者捅伤一位拉比
也比在旅馆房间的镜子前
看着自己好
就算被你们的文化
弄得神魂颠倒
也比那样好
　　勇敢的孩子们
　　站在坦克前
　　在神圣的土地上
　　　说着你们的语言
真不要脸，伟大的诗人们
我爱过去，也爱你们
但我一定要做点什么
来改变你们那愚蠢嗜血的
　　音乐
那除了上帝没人会真的喜欢
回去写你的日记

那样似乎更好[*]

那样似乎更好
当我第一次听到他讲
但现在送上另一边脸颊
时候已经太晚

那听上去像是真理
那样似乎更好
但今天选择弱者
你必须是个傻蛋

我怀疑他说了什么
我怀疑他说的意思
他似乎提到了爱
但接着又提到了死

最好保持沉默
看清自己的位置
举起杯中的血
试着说谢主仁慈

---

[*] 这首诗涉及一个著名的《圣经》故事"登山宝训",耶稣在山上教导众人,告诉他们弱者是有福的,因为"天国是他们的",还让他们"不要与恶人作对,有人打你的右脸,连左脸也转过来由他打"。

It Seemed the Better Way

It seemed the better way
When first I heard him speak
But now it's much too late
To turn the other cheek

It sounded like the truth
It seemed the better way
You'd have to be a fool
To choose the meek today

I wonder what it was
I wonder what it meant
He seemed to touch on love
But then he touched on death

Better hold my tongue
Better learn my place
Lift my glass of blood
Try to say the Grace

巨大的分裂

我从来都不喜欢你爱的方式
如此狡猾，如此陈旧
但我还是像个和尚那样斋戒
祈祷能看见你赤裸的身体

我看见你伤害每个人
一个残暴的统治者
我告诉自己"愿你的旨意实现
我的无足轻重"

我喝得太多我丢了工作
我活得好像什么都无所谓
而你，你从未出现
你甚至从未给我一个回答

这是盲目而破碎的时代
这个时代禁止仁慈
我猜我想要搭个便车
从迷幻剂到宗教

但所有导向灯都已熄灭
所有指示牌都已不见
我读的爱之书是错的
它有个快乐结局

然而当系统遭到冲击
变得面目全非
那些被我忘掉的简单事情
重新回到它们甜蜜的位置

我想我看见你带着一个孩子
我想我听见你在哭泣
你照看下的花园
一片繁茂安宁

我不记得后来发生了什么
我刻意与你保持距离
但纠缠于性爱之结
我的惩罚已经被取消

你的解药在我手里
你的手指在我发间
吻从我们唇上开始
抵达身体的每一处

而当我收拾好想要离开
你却把我拉到身边
要我做你夏娃的亚当
在巨大的分裂发生之前

被拴牢在这儿我们无法动弹
除了我们彼此之间
我们伸展我们沉溺犹如百合
从无处可去到世界中心

在这儿我无法轻易
去追踪美丽的线条
但线条还是被追踪
爱喜欢来去自由

在这儿无罪可认
也没有罪人要饶恕
有规定法律必须休息
在法律被写好之前

在这儿沉默被抹去
背景全部拆除
你的美无从比较
没有镜子，也没有影子

但现在它来了，一阵掠过的风
盲目而宁静

它割伤了我，当我分开你的唇
它割伤了我们，在你我之间

现在战争可以重新开始
那些折磨和笑声
在真理到达之前，和之后
我们高声哭喊，一如常人

我不知道这一切将如何结束
你总是让结局保持神秘
但哦，你是惟一
我从未觉得了解的朋友

THE GREAT DIVIDE

I never liked the way you loved
So devious, so dated
But still I fasted like a monk
And prayed to see you naked

I'd see you hurting everyone
A government of suffering
I'd tell myself 'Thy Will Be Done
My will it counts for nothing'

I drank a lot I lost my job
I lived like nothing mattered
And you, you never came across
You never even answered

It was a blind and broken time
And kindness was forbidden
I guess I tried to hitch a ride
From acid to religion

But every guiding light was gone
And every good direction
The book of love I read was wrong
It had a happy ending

But when the system had been shocked
Beyond all recognition
The simple things that I'd forgot
Resumed their sweet position

I thought I saw you with a child
I thought I heard you weeping
And all the garden round you wild
And safely in your keeping

I don't recall what happened next
I kept you at a distance
But tangled in the knot of sex
My punishment was lifted

Your remedies beneath my hand
Your fingers in my hair
The kisses on our lips began
That ended everywhere

And when I gathered up to leave
You drew me to your side
To be as Adam was to Eve
Before the Great Divide

And fastened here we cannot move
Except to one another
We spread and drown as lilies do
From nowhere to the centre

And here I cannot lift a hand
To trace the lines of beauty
But lines are traced and love is glad
To come and go so freely

And here no sin can be confessed
No sinner be forgiven
It's written that the law must rest
Before the law is written

And here the silence is erased
The background all dismantled
Your beauty cannot be compared
No mirror here, no shadow

But now it comes, a grazing wind
Aimless and serene
It wounds me as I part your lips
It wounds us in between

And now the wars can start anew
The torture and the laughter
We cry aloud, as humans do
Before the truth, and after

I don't know how it's going to end
You always left that open
But oh, you are the only friend
I never thought of knowing

现在我可以

现在我可以
一天睡二十个小时
剩下的四个小时
用来
给大人物
打电话
对他们说
晚安

天生就
让人发笑的
自闲
垂首

this feels good

September 6 2003
Los Angeles

感觉不错
2003年9月6日
洛杉矶

I Am Now Able

I am now able
to sleep twenty hours a day
The remaining four
are spent
telephoning a list
of important people
in order
to say goodnight

Jikan
who was born
to make men laugh
bows his head

流

你被告知
"要随波逐流"
但正如你
从学习中所知，
没有什么流，
事实上
没有来也没有去。
这些只是
对见习和尚
有用的概念。
你可以重新开始抽烟，
至于什么叫"你的死"
什么叫"你的生"
通过智慧的双眼
你现在可以看透。
这就是为什么
日本的智者
把他们的香烟命名为
"希望"与"和平"
以及"淡和平"与"短希望"
以及"淡的短希望"。

THE FLOW

You have been told to
"go with the flow"
but as you know
from your studies,
there is no flow,
nor is there actually
any coming or going.
These are merely
helpful concepts
for the novice monk.
You can start smoking again,
and what is called "your death"
and what is called "your life"
you can watch now
through the eyes of wisdom.
This is why
the Sages of Japan
named their cigarettes
"Hope" and "Peace"
and "Peace Light" and "Short Hope"
and "Short Hope Light."

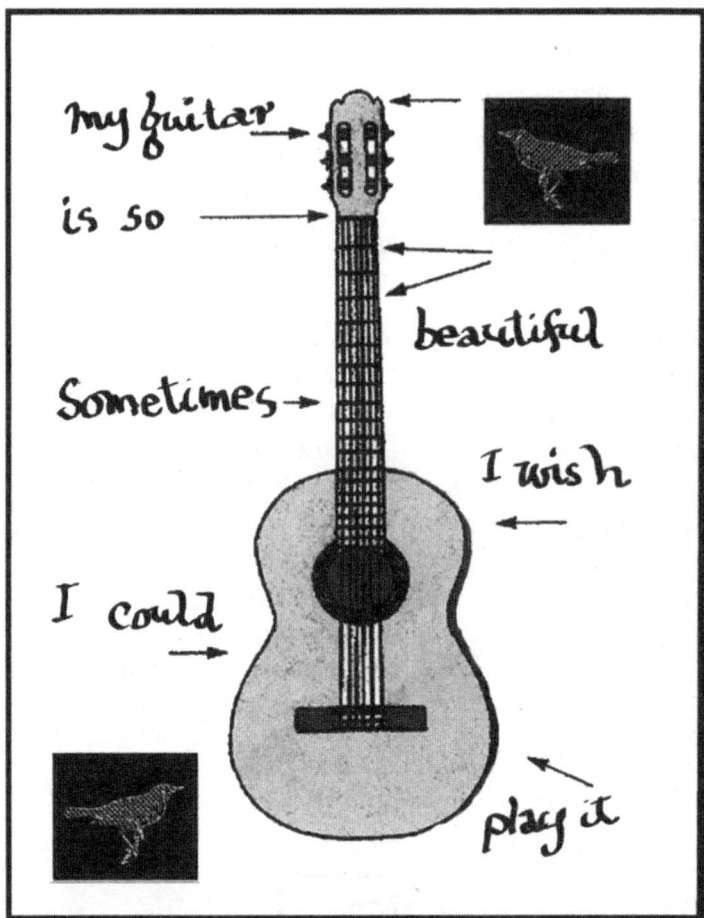

我的吉他　　我希望
如此　　　　我能
美丽　　　　弹它
有时

致中国读者的信

亲爱的读者：

　　谢谢你拿起这本书。能把我年轻时那些狂热的念头用中文来表达，是一种荣幸，也是一个惊喜。对于译者和出版方为把这部怪诞的作品介绍给你们所付出的努力，我表示由衷的感谢。我希望你们会觉得它有用，或者有趣。

　　当我年轻的时候，我和我的朋友们都读过并很崇拜中国古代的诗人。关于爱与友谊，酒与远方，以及诗歌本身，我们的观念都深受这些古老诗歌的影响。很久以后，在佐佐木承周老师指导下修习禅宗的那些年里，我每天都要研习令人激动的临济宗禅法。因此你可以理解，亲爱的读者，凭借如此浅薄的资格，能在你们的传统边缘掠过——哪怕只有片刻——我是感到多么的荣幸。

　　这是一本难读的书，即使是用英文，如果把它太当真的话。要我说，你不妨跳过那些你不喜欢的地方。随意浏览。说不定会有一段，或者甚至一页，能与你的好奇心产生共鸣。过一阵子，如果你实在无聊或没事干，也许你会想把它从头到尾地读完。不管怎样，我都要感谢你们，会对这样一个由爵士连复段，波普艺术笑话，宗教媚俗和闷声祈祷组成的大杂烩感兴趣，这种兴趣，在我看来，显得相当轻率，不过却非常感人，同时也表现出你们的宽容。

　　《美丽失败者》是在户外写的，在我海德拉岛的房子后面，一张摆在石头、野草和雏菊间的桌子上。海德拉岛是一座爱琴海上的小岛。很多年前我住在那儿。那是个酷热的夏天。我从没用东西遮过阳。你现在拿在手里的更像一份中暑记录，而不是一本书。

　　亲爱的读者，请原谅我，如果我浪费了你的时间。

A Note to the Chinese Reader

Dear Reader,

Thank you for coming to this book. It is an honour, and a surprise, to have the frenzied thoughts of my youth expressed in Chinese characters. I sincerely appreciate the efforts of the translator and the publishers in bringing this curious work to your attention. I hope you will find it useful or amusing.

When I was young, my friends and I read and admired the old Chinese poets. Our ideas of love and friendship, of wine and distance, of poetry itself, were much affected by those ancient songs. Much later, during the years when I practised as a Zen monk under the guidance of my teacher Kyozan Joshu Roshi, the thrilling sermons of Lin Chi (Rinzai) were studied every day. So you can understand, Dear Reader, how privileged I feel to be able to graze, even for a moment, and with such meagre credentials, on the outskirts of your tradition.

This is a difficult book, even in English, if it is taken too seriously. May I suggest that you skip over the parts you don't like? Dip into it here and there. Perhaps there will be a passage, or even a page, that resonates with your curiosity. After a while, if you are sufficiently bored or unemployed, you may want to read it from cover to cover. In any case, I thank you for your interest in this odd collection of jazz riffs, pop-art jokes, religious kitsch and muffled prayer, an interest which indicates, to my thinking, a rather reckless, though very touching, generosity on your part.

Beautiful Losers was written outside, on a table set among the rocks, weeds and daisies, behind my house on Hydra, an island in the Aegean Sea. I lived there many years ago. It was a blazing hot summer. I never covered my head. What you have in your hands is more of a sunstroke than a book.

Dear Reader, please forgive me if I have wasted your time.

We will
not be
staying
for the
entire
performance

01/01/04

我们不会整场演出都呆在那儿
04/01/01

信仰

海又深又暗
太阳，强烈的后悔
俱乐部，车轮，思想，
哦爱，你怎么还不累？

鲜血，泥土，信仰
这些词你不能忘
你的誓言，你的圣殿
哦爱，你怎么还不累？

每座山上的十字架
一颗星，一座宣礼塔*
这么多坟墓要填满
哦爱，你怎么还不累？

海又深又暗
但太阳仍在此落下
连时间自己都松开了
哦爱，你怎么还不累？

THE FAITH

The sea so deep and blind
The sun, the wild regret
The club, the wheel, the mind,
O love, aren't you tired yet?

The blood, the soil, the faith
These words you can't forget
Your vow, your holy place
O love, aren't you tired yet?

A cross on every hill
A star, a minaret
So many graves to fill
O love, aren't you tired yet?

The sea so deep and blind
Where still the sun must set
And time itself unwind
O love, aren't you tired yet?

---

* 宣礼塔（minaret），伊斯兰教清真寺的尖塔。

这是

这是你的皇冠
你的玉玺和指环
这是你的爱
给世间万物

这是你的推车
你的硬纸板和小便
这是你的爱
给所有这一切

愿人人都活着
愿人人都死去
你好，我的爱
我的爱，再见

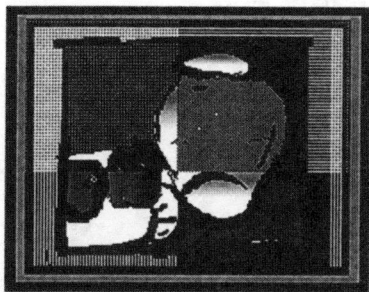

这是你的酒
你醉醺醺的堕落
这是你的爱
你爱的所有

这是你的病
你的马桶和床

这是你的爱
给女人，也给男人

这是夜晚
夜晚已经来临
这是你的死
在你儿子心中

这是黎明
（直到死亡把我们分开）
这是你的死
在你女儿心中

这是你在赶路
这是你已离去
这是爱
一切都建于其上

这是你的十字架
你的钉子和山丘
这是你的爱
标明了要向何方

愿人人都活着
愿人人都死去
你好，我的爱
我的爱，再见

HERE IT IS

Here is your crown
and your seal and rings
and here is your love
for all things

Here is your cart
your cardboard and piss
and here is your love
for all of this

May everyone live
and may everyone die
Hello, my love
and my love, Goodbye

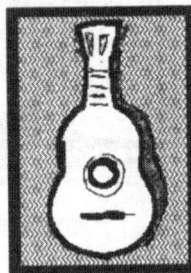

Here is your wine
and your drunken fall
and here is your love
your love for it all

Here is your sickness
your bed and your pan
and here is your love
for the woman, the man

And here is the night
the night has begun
and here is your death
in the heart of your son

and here is the dawn
(until death do us part)
and here is your death
in your daughter's heart

And here you are hurried
and here you are gone
and here is the love
that it's all built upon
Here is your cross
your nails and your hill
and here is your love
that lists where it will

May everyone live
and may everyone die
Hello, my love
and my love, Goodbye

担心　　　感恩
　当然　　　当然

失败　　　自从
当然　　　背景
　　　　消失以后

老了
当然

为你而来

当一切崩溃
当心如刀割
我现在明白
我为你而来

别问我为什么
我知道这是真的
我现在明白
我为你而来

像以往一样
我制订计划
可当我回望
我为你而来

像平常一样
我走在街上
我吓得发呆
但我为你而来

我从头回顾
我的人生
那从未是我
那一直是你

你派我去这儿
你派我去那儿
弄坏很多
我修不好的东西

做出很多
精神产品
做出更多
不假思索

吃饭
喝酒
我还以为这副皮囊
归我所有

扮成阿拉伯人
扮成犹太人
哦，铁面人
我为你而来

荣耀之情
邪恶之情
世界浸透了
血淋淋的毛巾

死还是老样子
但它永远常新
我吓得发呆
我为你而来

我心里清楚
我一直明白
那从未是我
我为你而来

我为你而来
我的亲爱
在你统治下
一切都是尘埃

别问我为什么
我知道这是真的
我现在明白
我为你而来

THERE FOR YOU

When it all went down
And the pain came through
I get it now
I was there for you

Don't ask me how
I know it's true
I get it now
I was there for you

I make my plans
Like I always do
But when I look back
I was there for you

I walk the streets
Like I used to do
And I freeze with fear
But I'm there for you

I see my life
In full review
It was never me
It was always you

You sent me here
You sent me there
Breaking things
I can't repair

Making objects
Out of thought
Making more
By thinking not

Eating food
And drinking wine
A body that
I thought was mine

Dressed as arab
Dressed as jew
O mask of iron
I was there for you

Moods of glory
Moods so foul
The world comes through
A bloody towel

And death is old
But it's always new
I freeze with fear
And I'm there for you

I see it clear
I always knew
It was never me
I was there for you

I was there for you
My darling one
And by your law
It all was done

Don't ask me how
I know it's true
I get it now
I was there for you

承诺

A PROMISE

我绝不会
把圣杯
还给
它的
"合法主人"

I will never
return
the Holy Grail
to its
"rightful owners."

furthermore, you do not have the legitimate authority to examine me

再说，你并没有合法的权力来审查我

向R.S.B.*汇报

平静没有进入我的生活。
我的生活逃走了
　　　而平静还在那儿。
我常常碰见我的生活，
当它想歇口气，
付账单，
或忍受那些新闻，
当它一如既往
被某人
　　　美的缆绳绊倒——
我小小的生活：
如此忠诚
如此执着于它那模糊的目标——
而且，我急忙汇报说，
没有我也干得很好。

REPORT TO R.S.B.

Peace did not come into my life.
My life escaped
　　　and peace was there.
Often I bump into my life,
trying to catch its breath,
pay a bill,
or tolerate the news,
tripping as usual
over the cables
　　　of someone's beauty –
My little life:
so loyal,
so devoted to its obscure purposes –
And, I hasten to report,
doing fine without me.

* R.S.B是Ramesh S. Balsekar（1917—2009）的缩写，印度圣人萨伽达塔·马哈拉吉的门徒，著名的不二论哲学大师。

欧文和我在医院

他支持尼采
我支持基督
他支持胜利
我支持失败

我爱读他的诗
他爱听我的歌
我们从没什么兴趣
争论谁对谁错

他打拳的手在颤抖
他在跟烟斗搏斗
那是我帮他点燃的
帝王牌烟丝

IRVING AND ME AT THE HOSPITAL

He stood up for Nietzsche
I stood up for Christ
He stood up for victory
I stood up for less

I loved to read his verses
He loved to hear my song
We never had much interest
In who was right or wrong

His boxer's hands were shaking
He struggled with his pipe
Imperial Tobacco
Which I helped him light

IRVING

– *after the photo by Laszlo*

欧文
——据拉兹罗所拍照片

sit still
and let
them
examine
you

February
7th
2005

坐着不动
让
他们
检查

你

2005年2月7日

still looking
at the girls
but there are
no girls
none at all
there is only
(this'll kill ya)
inner peace
& harmony

the evening in the hotel   1/7/03

还在看
女孩
但根本
没有女孩
一个都没有
只有
（这会害死你）
内心的平静
与和谐

旅馆之夜 03/1/7

就因为几首歌

就因为几首歌
歌中我唱出了她们的谜，
于是女人们
对我的年老
格外客气。
她们在忙碌的生活中
辟出一块秘密角落
并把我带到那里。
她们用不同的方式
赤身裸体
她们还说，
　"看着我，莱昂纳德
再看我最后一眼。"
接着她们就扑到床上
覆盖住我
像个颤抖的婴儿。

BECAUSE OF A FEW SONGS

Because of a few songs
wherein I spoke of their mystery,
women have been
exceptionally kind
to my old age.
They make a secret place
in their busy lives
and they take me there.
They become naked
in their different ways
and they say,
"Look at me, Leonard
look at me one last time."
Then they bend over the bed
and cover me up
like a baby that is shivering.

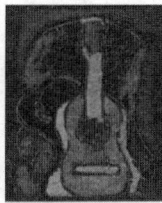

信

你一直不喜欢
我寄给你的信。
但现在你终于明白
我信中意思的要领。

你开始重新阅读
那些你没烧掉的信。
你把它们印上你的唇，
页页都是我的忧虑。

我说发过一次洪灾。
之后什么都没留下。
我希望你能来。
我给你我的地址。

你的故事太长，
情节又太紧张，
你花了多年才越过
自我保护的坎。

受伤的形式显现：
失去的东西，彻底的程度；
还有这简洁的亲切，
有力的孤独。

你走进我的房间。
你坐到我的桌前，
开始写信给
下一个来者。

THE LETTERS

You never liked to get
The letters that I sent.
But now you've got the gist
Of what my letters meant.

You're reading them again,
The ones you didn't burn.
You press them to your lips,
My pages of concern.

I said there'd been a flood.
I said there's nothing left.
I hoped that you would come.
I gave you my address.

Your story was so long,
The plot was so intense,
It took you years to cross
The lines of self-defence.

The wounded forms appear:
the loss, the full extent;
and simple kindness here,
the solitude of strength.

You walk into my room.
You sit there at my desk,
Begin your letter to
The one who's coming next.

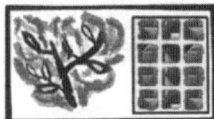

only one thing
made him happy
and now that
it was gone
everything
made him happy

September 27, 2004
Montréal

只有一件事
能让他开心
既然这件事
不行了
所有事
都让他开心

2004年9月27日
蒙特利尔

餐桌

同样的无用念头又升起
但无人将它们认领——
孤独抓住画框
抖掉了希望
但没有人没有希望
也没有人感到孤独——
为下一刻
所做的复杂准备
指引你
去读这段话——
任由主的摆布
他把我放到这儿
我坐在这张桌旁
大约四十年前
那些歌
正是从这里开始——
忙碌得像只
寂寞的蜜蜂

——海德拉岛，1999

KITCHEN TABLE

The same useless thoughts arise
but no one claims them –
Loneliness seizes the frame
and shakes away hope
but no one is hopeless
no one is lonely –
The intricate preparations
for the next moment
direct you
to read this now –
Surrendered to the One
who placed me here
I sit at the very table
where these songs began
some forty years ago –
busy as a bee
in the solitude

> – *Hydra, 1999*

万有引力

我从没想过要看你的脸，
我也不想知道
那个我必将要去的
地下某处的细节。

但爱像万有引力一般强劲，
每个人都必须坠落。

最初是从苹果树，
然后从西方的墙。

最初是从苹果树，
然后从西方的墙。
然后从你，然后从我
然后从我们大家。

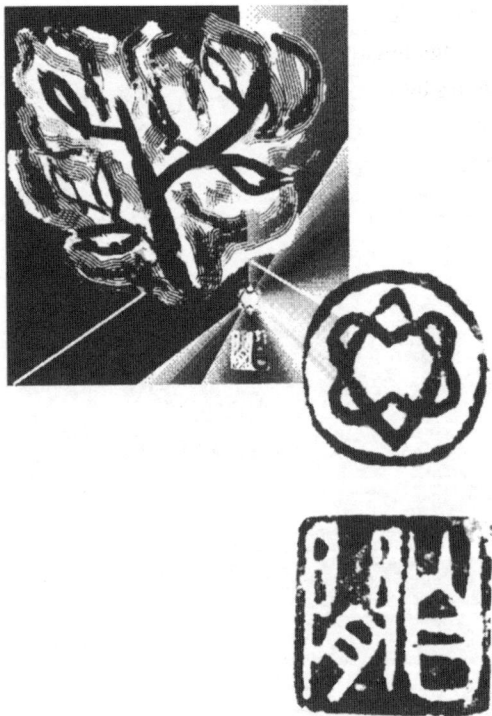

GRAVITY

I never tried to see your face,
Nor did I want to know
The details of some lower place
Where I would have to go.

But love is strong as gravity,
And everyone must fall.
At first it's from the apple tree,
And then the western wall.

At first it's from the apple tree,
And then the western wall.
And then from you and then from me
And then from one and all

太阳

我曾去过太阳
那儿没什么特别
一个暴力的地方
很像我们地球

太阳说
我是一本打开的书
耐心点

你会发现
不管在哪里
所有事情
都以同样的方式发生

太阳风
则是另一码事
没人能控制它们
没人能真正
驾驭它们

你要么活下来
要么从此
音讯全无

我喜欢太阳
说话的方式
如此镇静而坦诚
除非它被自己的不幸
一把抓住

THE SUN

I've been to the sun
It's nothing special
A place of violence
Much like our own

The sun said
I am an open book
Be patient

You will find
That everything happens
The same way
Here and there

The solar winds
Are something else
No one masters them
No one really
Navigates them

You survive them
Or you are never
Heard from again

I love the way
The sun speaks
It is so calm and honest
Except when seized
By its own misfortunes

很快\就没人\画\我了\因为\我没有\哦\我艺术中\神秘的\不精确

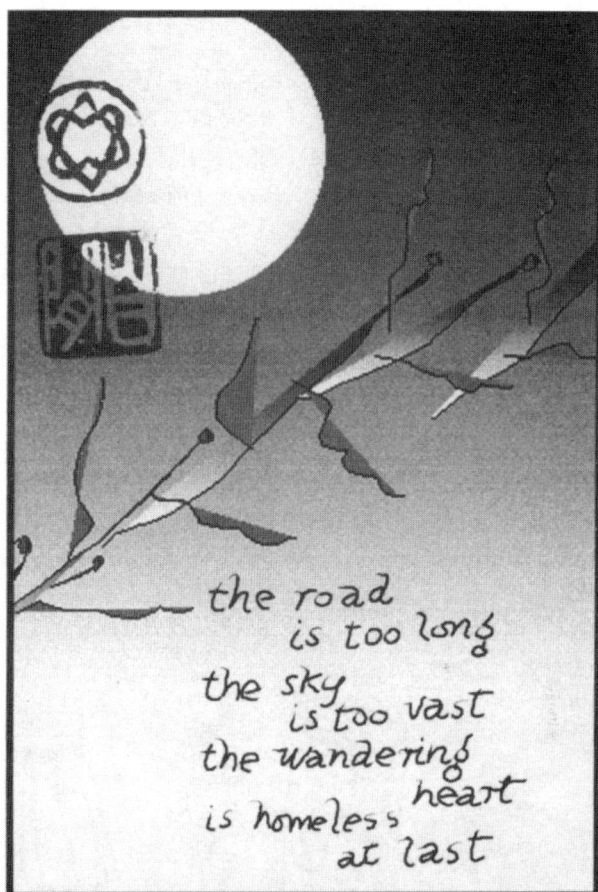

the road
is too long
the sky
is too vast
the wandering
heart
is homeless
at last

路
　太长
天
　太大
流浪的

心
最终
无家可归

去吧，小书

去吧，小书
躲起来
为你的胡言乱语
感到羞愧

一次侥幸
让你变得出名
而你本来
要很晚
才会被发现

要等到再也没有
洪水，地震
和圣战

去吧，小书
别再给我丢脸
我生活中有许多
严肃的男女
你让他们
占了上风

去躲到
一扇窗后面
哦，我亲爱的
快乐而率真的
小书
或者把自己碾碎
在失败脚下

但先躲
快躲
然后用秘密暗号
跟我联络
那暗号就像
一种严重的咳嗽

那黑暗的咳声
无视
爱的挑战
完美的结晶
哦，从你藏身的
那些地方
对我说话

去吧，小书
然后邀请我去你那儿

GO LITTLE BOOK

Go little book
And hide
And be ashamed
Of your irrelevance

A fluke
Has made you prominent
You were meant
To be discovered
Later

When there are no more
Floods and earthquakes
And holy wars

Go little book
And stop disgracing me
There are serious men
And women in my life
And you have given them
The upper hand

Hide behind
A window

O my dear lighthearted
And transparent
Book
Or crush yourself
Beneath a defeat

But hide
Hide quickly now
And let me hear from you
In our secret code
Which resembles
A bad cough

That dark rattle
Which ignores
The challenges of love
The crystals of perfection

O speak to me
From places
You will find

Go little book
Invite me there

客气

跟一个老头
喝干邑白兰地——
　　在河边简陋的小屋
他非同一般的客气——
也就是，不客气
只管把酒瓶在我杯子里倒空
把我的盘子堆满
在我要走的时候
酣然入睡

HOSPITALITY

drinking cognac
with the old man –
　　his exquisite hospitality
in the shack by the river –
that is, no hospitality
just emptying the bottle into my glass
and filling my plate
and falling asleep
when it was time to go

中心

当我处于
暗恋的中心
我无法把它当成一样东西
它没有折磨人的
锋利棱角
我呼吸着那渴望
散发的芬芳
而那渴望
没有主人
当夜晚从星座中
挑挑拣拣
为取悦
莱昂纳德的真爱
把项链放下
又拿起
"哦，我的爱"
这呼唤拥抱着
无边的天空
"哦，我的爱"
每一片雪花都在呼喊
而森林
也从很高的地方回应：
"哦，我的爱"
于是一颗心出现
于是一颗心融化
暴风雪中
我被困的地方
它们紧抱在一起
我走向你
踩着欲望的波涛

走过长长的距离
我有新的事情要告诉你
关于你的美丽
你迷人的双腿
以及你无情的离开

The Centre

When I am at the centre
of my unrequited love
I cannot hold it as an object
It has no sharp edges
to torture anyone
I breathe the fragrance
of the longing
and the longing
has no proprietor
"O my love" embraces
the great wide sky
as the night picks through
the constellations
lifting necklace
after dripping necklace
for the delight
of Leonard's true beloved

"O my love" cries out
from every pore of snow
and the forest answers
from a great height:
"O my love"
And one heart appears
and one heart dissolves
and they clasp in the place
where I am held up
in the storm
And I walk to you
on the waves of desire
walk across the distance
with something new to tell you
about your beauty
your good legs
and your relentless absence

你对新观点的胃口永不满足

当你想要
在不同的光线下
看她
你便把她
放到我怀里

当你想要
松一口气
暂时消失
你便让她的唇
转向我的唇

哦，主宰一切的
无名的神
你赐了一首歌

给我幽灵般的人生

你对自身的渴望
是多么深切
多么壮观的俯瞰

我们在感恩中跪下
当爱中的动作
穿过虚构的
"陪伴"
驱散了我们甜蜜的意图——
两个生物
"你"这样叫"我"

（孔亚雷　译）

YOUR RELENTLESS APPETITE
FOR NEW PERSPECTIVES

When You wanted
to see her
in a different light
You placed her
in my arms

When You wanted
to vanish
in a sigh of relief
You drew down her lips
to mine

O Nameless Subject
of all activity

You have given me a song
for my ghostly life

How deep is Your longing
for Yourself
how sublimely overlooked

We kneel in gratitude
as the movements in love
disperse our sweet intentions
across the fictions
of Companionship –
two of the creatures
which You named Me

迷失更好

我迷失时更好
一个个城镇流过
像电视
你想当艺术家
画女侍嘴唇

我醒来时更好
独在冰冷桑拿室
重新认知树木
红木，雪松
老橡木桶
旧十字架

噢我的孩子，迷失
更好，当你是
女人的爱情盛宴
中毒的父亲
我没带你
猎熊
或叉鱼
我没把你
从风流韵事
拐到森林绿中
在那里我和
叫撒哈拉*的睡觉

在魔鬼河**边
我知道如何
在风中搭帐篷

迷失更好
按CNN的恐怖
睡觉
喝红酒烂醉
挖掘阳光
在永不变英文的
德国文献片中

是血更好
在我自己手中
带上它甜蜜生活
和天真快乐的
工作负担
噢感谢亲密的
我手的忠诚之血
我保证发怒时
不再举起你

（北岛　译）

---

* 撒哈拉指撒哈拉沙漠。
** 魔鬼河（Devil's River）在美国得克萨斯州。

326

BETTER TO BE LOST

It is better when I'm lost
and the towns flow by
like television
and you want to be an artist
and draw the waitress's lips
📺 📺 📺 📺 📺 📺 📺 📺 📺 📺
💋 💋 💋 💋 💋 💋 💋 💋 💋 💋
It is better when I wake up
alone in the cold sauna
and get to know the wood again
the red wood, the cedar
the old oaken bucket
the old rugged cross
✝ ✝ ✝ ✝ ✝ ✝ ✝ ✝ ✝ ✝ ✝ ✝ ✝ ✝

👁 👁 👁 👁 👁 👁 👁 👁 👁 👁 👁
O my children it is better
to be lost when you are
this poisoned father
at the woman's banquet of love
and I did not take you
to hunt the bear
or spear the fish
I did not spirit you away
from the intrigue
to the forest green
where I slept with

a person named Sahara
beside The Devil's River
and I knew how to put up
a tent in the wind
🕷 🕷 🕷 🕷 🕷 🕷 🕷 🕷 🕷 🕷 🕷 🕷 🕷
It is better to be lost
to fall asleep according
to the terrors of CNN
dead drunk on red wine
digging for the sunlight
in the German documentary
that never turns into English
🍾 🍾 🍾 🍾 🍾 🍾 🍾 🍾 🍾 🍾 🍾 🍾 🍾 🍾 🍾 🍾 🍾
📺 📺 📺 📺 📺 📺 📺 📺 📺 📺 📺
It is better to be the blood
inside my own hand
with its own sweet life
its innocent joyous burden
of service
O thank you dear sweet
loyal blood of my hand
I promise never to raise you
again in anger
💋 💋 💋 💋 💋 💋 💋 💋 💋 💋
✝ ✝ ✝ ✝ ✝ ✝ ✝ ✝ ✝ ✝ ✝ ✝ ✝ ✝ ✝ ✝
👁 👁 👁 👁 👁 👁 👁 👁 👁 👁 👁

在我们的爱里

现在我想爱你
然后我还想爱你
我再也不想爱你
于是又重新开始

当你从那高处
弯腰笑我的时候
我腰带上的流苏
全都飞向空中

我想成为小丑
就是你每隔一天
用完就扔的
那种

我想成为玫瑰
你打着哈欠招手
挂着多刺的拐杖
穿过草坪的火热

看看你对我做了什么
好像你一点都不在乎
我曾有自己的底线
但如今早已越过

我不会回来跟你说再见
我永远不会离开你身边
直到我成为另一个男人
直到你成为别人的新娘

坐到我的记忆上
当你感到痛苦
当你感到快乐
也坐上去吧

承蒙你的好意
谢谢你的醉吻
其实我醉得比你厉害
但我不想告诉你

每个夜晚都被水泥密封
直到你奋起反抗
像汹涌海潮挟带着我
冲破谎言之墙

并把我永远抛入地下
我在那里找到
我情同手足的化石
那些软体和脊椎动物

而后神圣的一刻降临
带着绝对的清醒：
我意识到我们注定为枷锁而生
纵然每个原子都很自由

我意识到我们注定为枷锁而生
纵然每个原子都很自由
正如你可以清楚地看见
即使美也有一个极限

于是夏天有你的金发
秋天有你的幽灵
我们来到一场狂欢的盛宴
在那儿谁也不是主人

于是我们又开始成形
这需要花一点时间
我绕着你的隐私打转
跑了许多寂寞的里程

INSIDE OUR LOVE

I want to love you now
I want to love you then
I want to love you never
And then begin again

All the tassels of my belt
Go flying in the sky
When you bend down to laugh at me
From your place on high

I want to be the fool
The one you send away
After you have used him up
Every second day

I want to be the rose
You beckon with a yawn
Limping on a thorny crutch
Across the burning lawn

See what you have done to me
As if you give a shit
I used to live behind a line
But now I'm over it

I won't come back to say goodbye
I'll never leave your side
Until I am the other man
And you are someone's bride

Sit down on my memory
When you are in pain
When you are in pleasure
Sit down on it again

Thank you for your courtesy

And for your drunken kiss
I'm drunker than you'll ever be
I hate to tell you this
And every night's cemented tight
Until you strike and rise
Against me like a tidal flood
To crack the wall of lies

And push me down forever
To places where I find
The fossils of my brotherhood
The smooth ones and the spined

And then a holy moment comes
With crisp sobriety:
I see that we are meant for chains
Though every atom's free

I see that we are meant for chains
Tho' every atom's free
And even beauty meets an edge
As one can plainly see

Then summer has your golden hair
And autumn has your ghost
And we are at a juicy feast
Where no one is the host

Then we begin to form again
It takes a little while
I circle round your privacy
For many a lonesome mile

I copied time
I knew I was a fiction
but I could not suspend myself

Moving back
or going forward
I encountered
no obstacles

I carried mountains
leaves fell inside me

I surrounded
your beauty
with applause

and when
you wanted to go home
I swept aside the infant dust

我复制时间
我知道我是虚构的
但我无法自己停止

往后退
或向前走
我一路

毫无障碍

我扛着群山
树叶落入我的身体

我用喝彩
环绕

你的美

而当你
想要回家
我会拂去那初生的尘埃

but turn me on my side
so I can better see

that dear expanse

of grassy lawn

where on she

walked, or

should I

say,

floated,

yes, floated
under the
sunfilled
sail of her parasol

2/4/03

但请把我转向那边
这样我就能更好地看见
那片可爱宽敞的
绿草坪，她正在上面
散步，或者
也许

我应该说，
漂浮，
是的，漂浮在
她那
充满阳光的
阳伞帆下　03/2/4

3号房里的灯

（3号房里的灯　圣安妮旅馆）
很奇妙，不是吗?
　在这家
吕贝隆附近的
圣安妮旅馆，
　由我来宣告
人类孤独的结束
我觉得这很奇妙

谁能想到
我会是那个
在这家旅馆宣告
　人类孤独结束
的人呢
人类的孤独
就在这家旅馆

这是最甜蜜的职责
由我来宣告
这条新闻：我
正在
　　等待
人类孤独的结束

1980

334

THE LAMP IN ROOM 3

CURIOUS, was it not?
   it fell on me to
proclaim, from this hotel

Hotel Ste. Anne beside
   the **L**UBERON,
the end of human solitude
I find it curious

who ever thought
that I would be the
one to proclaim
   the end of human
solitude ~~from this hotel~~
human solitude
~~from this hotel~~

the sweetest duty
to proclaim
   the news that I
myself
   was waiting for
the end of human soli
Of human solitude

1980

半个世界

每晚她都来找我
我给她做饭，给她倒茶
那时她三十多岁
赚了点钱，有过几个男人
在白色的蚊帐里
我们一起躺下，互相给予，互相获取
因为没人去数
我们一载仿佛活了千年
烛光摇曳，月亮西沉
发亮的山丘，乳白的小镇
透明，轻盈，闪烁，
露出我们俩
在那片本性的大地，
在那儿，爱没有意识，没有束缚，自由自在
在那儿，我们发现了半个完美的世界

HALF THE WORLD

Every night she'd come to me
I'd cook for her, I'd pour her tea
She was in her thirties then
had made some money, lived with men
We'd lay us down to give and get
beneath the white mosquito net
And since no counting had begun
we lived a thousand years in one
The candles burned, the moon went down
the polished hill, the milky town
transparent, weightless, luminous,
uncovering the two of us
on that fundamental ground,
where love's unwilled, unleashed, unbound
and half the perfect world is found

硬撑
蒙特利尔，2003年11月19日

作弊

我做爱时作弊
她觉得很棒
她给我看
你只会给作弊者
看的东西

CHEATER

I cheat when I make love
She thinks it's great
She shows me stuff
that you'd only show
to a cheater

洪水

洪水它在聚集
很快就会到来
穿过所有山谷
掀翻所有屋顶
身体将会沉没
而灵魂将会解脱
我写下这一切
但我没有证据

——西奈山，1973

THE FLOOD

The flood it is gathering
Soon it will move
Across every valley
Against every roof
The body will drown
And the soul will break loose
I write all this down
But I don't have the proof

– Sinai, 1973

致谢

这些诗和画有很多最早出现在"莱昂纳德·科恩档案"上（www.leonardcohenfiles.com），一个非常出色的芬兰网站，由Jarkko Arjatsalo创设，并由他的儿子Rauli提供技术协助。我由衷感谢Arjatsalo一家，以及网站管理者Marie Mazur，Tomislav Sakic和Patrice Clos为我的作品所付出的非凡努力。

这本书里的有些作品后来成了歌词，由Sharon Robinson和我共同创作并演唱。这些歌你可以在索尼公司发行的CD《十首新歌》中听到。

多伦多的《Walrus》杂志好心地刊登了书中的一些诗和画，还有一些被翻译成克罗地亚语，刊登在萨格勒布的《Oris》杂志。

在和佐佐木承周老师及Ramesh S. Balsekar共度的珍贵时光中，我聆听了很多有趣而精辟的见解，之后我把它们融入了诗中。他们那些深邃的理念我领会得如此肤浅，所以人们不能指责我剽窃或吸取了他们的想法。

感谢我在多伦多和纽约的编辑，Ellen Seligman 和Dan Halpern，感谢他们在家中对我的盛情款待，感谢M&S公司的Marilyn Biderman仔细地将本书介绍给别处的出版社。
感谢Sam Feldman，Steve Macklam和Michelle Findlay扶我过马路。

感谢Adam，Lorca Cohen和Jessica Murphy在安息日的陪伴。
感谢我妹妹Esther Cohen的热情支持。

我还想表达我对Robert Kory，Michelle Rice和Anjani Thomas的感激之情，感谢他们的忠实，感谢他们亲切而熟练的导航。

再一次感谢Anjani。

谢谢老师
谢谢大家

（孔亚雷　译）

Acknowledgments

Many of these poems and drawings first appeared in The Leonard Cohen Files (www.leonardcohenfiles.com), a remarkable website out of Finland mastered by Jarkko Arjatsalo, with the technical assistance of his son Rauli. I am deeply grateful to the Arjatsalo family, and to the webmasters Marie Mazur, Tomislav Sakic, and Patrice Clos for their extraordinary efforts on behalf of my work.

Some of the pieces in this book became lyrics for songs that Sharon Robinson and I wrote and sang together. They can be heard on the Sony CD called *Ten New Songs*.

The *Walrus* magazine, out of Toronto, graciously published some poems and drawings, as did *Oris*, out of Zagreb, with Croatian translations.

I heard many interesting and precise ideas, which later I blurred into verse, while in the precious company of Kyozan Joshu Roshi, and Ramesh S. Balsekar. Their compelling concepts were so imperfectly grasped that I cannot be accused either of stealing or absorbing them.

I thank my editors in Toronto and New York, Ellen Seligman and Dan Halpern, for the wide hospitality of their houses, and Marilyn Biderman of M&S for carefully presenting this book to publishers elsewhere.
I thank Sam Feldman, Steve Macklam and Michelle Findlay for helping me across the street.

I thank Adam and Lorca Cohen and Jessica Murphy for their Sabbath company.
I thank my sister Esther Cohen for her exuberant support.

I want to express my gratitude to Robert Kory, Michelle Rice, and Anjani Thomas for their loyalty and their kind and skilful navigations.

And to Anjani, again.

Thank you, Teachers
Thank you, Everyone

Leonard Cohen
BOOK OF LONGING
Copyright © 2006 by Leonard Cohen
Chinese Simplified Characters Copyright © 2020
By Shanghai Translation Publishing House
Bilingual English and Simplified Chinese language edition published in agreement with McClelland & Stewart Ltd.,
through The Grayhawk Agency
All rights reserved

图字：09 – 2011 – 636号

图书在版编目（CIP）数据

渴望之书 /（加）莱昂纳德·科恩（Leonard Cohen）著；孔亚雷，北岛译. —上海：上海译文出版社，2020.12
（莱昂纳德·科恩作品）
书名原文：Book of Longing
ISBN 978－7－5327－8630－5

Ⅰ.①渴… Ⅱ.①莱…②孔…③北… Ⅲ.①诗集－加拿大－现代 Ⅳ.①I711.25

中国版本图书馆CIP数据核字（2020）第251499号

渴望之书（中英对照/图文珍藏本）
[加拿大] 莱昂纳德·科恩 著 孔亚雷 北岛 译
策划 / 冯涛 责任编辑 / 管舒宁 装帧设计 / 胡枫

上海译文出版社有限公司出版、发行
网址：www.yiwen.com.cn
200001 上海福建中路193号
苏州市越洋印刷有限公司印刷

开本890×1240 1/32 印张11.5 插页6 字数160,000
2021年4月第1版 2021年4月第1次印刷
印数：0,001—7,000册

ISBN 978－7－5327－8630－5/I·5329
定价：76.00元